Ophelia

First edition published in French under the title *Ophélie* by la courte échelle
Copyright © 2008 by Les éditions de la courte échelle inc.
English translation copyright © 2018 by Christelle Morelli and Susan Ouriou
First published in English translation in Canada and the USA in 2018 by Groundwood Books

Groundwood Books / House of Anansi Press
groundwoodbooks.com

We acknowledge for their financial support of our publishing program the Canada Council for the Arts, the Ontario Arts Council and the Government of Canada.

We acknowledge the financial support of the Government of Canada through the National Translation Program for Book Publishing, an initiative of the *Roadmap for Canada's Official Languages 2013-2018: Education, Immigration, Communities*, for our translation activities.

 Canada Council for the Arts   Conseil des Arts du Canada

 ONTARIO ARTS COUNCIL
CONSEIL DES ARTS DE L'ONTARIO
an Ontario government agency
un organisme du gouvernement de l'Ontario

With the participation of the Government of Canada
Avec la participation du gouvernement du Canada | Canadä

Library and Archives Canada Cataloguing in Publication
Gingras, Charlotte
[Ophélie. English]
Ophelia / Charlotte Gingras ; [illustrated by] Daniel Sylvestre ; [translated by] Christelle Morelli, Susan Ouriou.
Translation of: Ophélie.
Issued in print and electronic formats.
ISBN 978-1-77306-099-6 (hardcover).—ISBN 978-1-77306-100-9 (HTML).—ISBN 978-1-77306-101-6 (Kindle)
I. Sylvestre, Daniel, illustrator II. Morelli, Christelle, translator III. Ouriou, Susan, translator IV. Title. V. Title: Ophélie. English.
PS8563.I598O6313 2018   jC843'.54   C2017-905301-9
C2017-905302-7

Jacket illustration by Daniel Sylvestre
Jacket design by Michael Solomon

Printed and bound in Canada

Ophelia
Charlotte Gingras

Illustrations by
Daniel Sylvestre

Translated by
Christelle Morelli and Susan Ouriou

Groundwood Books / House of Anansi Press
Toronto Berkeley

PART ONE
Broken Hearts

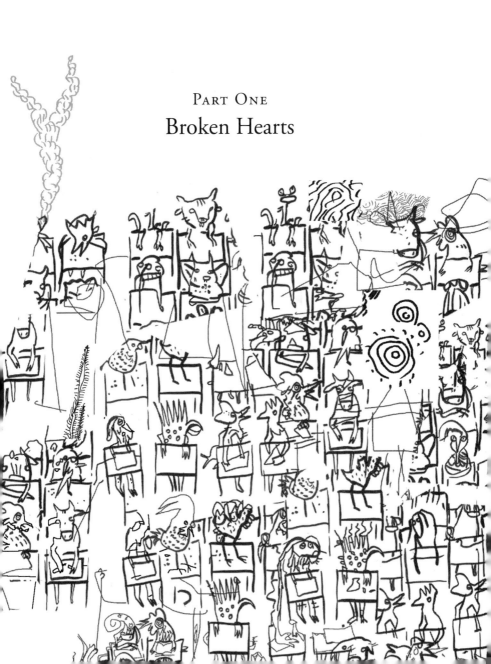

Hello, Jeanne,

Do you remember me? From this morning in the library?

I went with my French class, thirty grade-ten students looking like a herd of sheep heading for slaughter, heads down and feet dragging. Chairs were set up in rows at the back of the library and a table with a stack of books and a glass of water. You, the writer, stood next to the table. You had gray hair and the look of someone who'd ended up at the wrong address.

The guys dropped into random chairs, with their too-big bodies and giant feet. The girls yawned, played with their hair and chattered away about their weekend. Except me, wearing my layers of dark colors, sitting at the very back, alone. They call me rag girl. I pretend not to hear.

The librarian, beside herself with excitement because she adores books and authors so much, called out, "Quiet! We're about to start!"

Once the silence had stretched on long enough, you decided to speak, and in a voice so soft it almost wasn't there, you said, "My name is Jeanne D'Amour. I was invited by your school to talk about writing and reading. I could tell you what my work consists of and read excerpts from my books, but I'd rather you asked questions, I'd get a better idea of what interests you …"

Naturally, no one said a thing. Don't you know, Jeanne, that grade-ten students on a Monday morning have more in common with shell-less mollusks than human beings? You didn't budge, all alone, waiting. I didn't even raise my hand. My voice escaped, all claws, "Why do you write? What's the point in writing?"

The whole class turned to the last row of chairs, and the librarian looked ready to jump in. You stopped her with a gesture, smiled at me, and wrinkles formed around your pale eyes and down your cheeks.

"I write because I can't help myself. I write out of necessity. I'm inhabited by a character. Slowly the character develops inside me, like a fetus growing. Sometimes it doesn't make it to term, other times it does."

We stared at each other, you and I, our eyes locked for a second, maybe two or twenty-five. A stillness, a vaporous stillness that made a lot of the herd uneasy.

In the middle of that giant lull, a too-fat kid, a new guy, raised his hand. "Last summer, I wrote postcards to myself on my holiday by the sea."

The herd burst out laughing. Choked from laughing so hard. He turned a violent red. He couldn't disappear. His body took up too much space.

"Me too," you said, looking at him like you were the only two people on planet Earth. "I've been known to send myself postcards. When I got home, it felt like someone had been thinking of me."

The class of idiots froze. At the back, I silently screamed, "Do it! Don't stop! Help him if you can! Can you do it, writer woman?"

You kept soothing him, comforting him, because he was fat, ugly and friendless. "That's how it starts — writing, painting, music. Always. Because of an intolerable emptiness."

The others woke up then, and quietly and with incredible patience, you answered all their questions, even the dumb ones along the lines of "Can you make a lot of money writing? No? Why don't you write bestsellers? Why don't you write for TV? Do you write horror stories?"

The more time passed, the less shy you seemed and the rosier your cheeks got. You spoke of books with great tenderness. "They entertain us, teach us new things, awaken our curiosity, let us travel to other worlds, imaginary yet so close by. Sometimes a book lifts us up so high that we don't want to come back down, we put off the ending."

And then, after one of your silences, "Some books help us grieve. Or even save us from death."

You looked in turn at the fat boy and the girl with all her layers, the entirety of your fan club. Your lips trembled slightly. "That's it, I'm done."

The others clapped and left, dragging their feet and chattering. Forgetting. The postcard kid screwed up the courage to ask for your autograph. You scribbled a few words for him. He ran off, still red, mired in his rolls. You gathered together your own books that you hadn't even talked about. I was the only one left, still sitting in the back row. I got up and inched toward you, as skittish as an alley cat.

"Thank you," you said.

"For what?" I asked, taken aback.

"Thank you for helping me. Asking the first question is hard."

I shrugged. I hadn't asked my question to warm up the room. I couldn't care less about the others. The question needed to be asked, that's all. Then I stammered, "You didn't name the books that could save us from death."

Our eyes met again, like flashing swords, flying sparks, darts.

"I think everyone has to discover those books on their own. Sometimes you even have to write them yourself … Do you write?"

"No! I …"

I stopped. You hesitated — maybe you had something to add, but you didn't dare. In the end, you murmured, "What's your name?"

"Umm … Ophelia."

"Well, then … Goodbye, Ophelia."

I took a step back. You grabbed my hand. Yours was hot and dry. "Wait!"

From your bag, you pulled out a large notebook made of recycled paper with an ink-blue cover. Brand new, thick. On the first page, you wrote down your name and address in block letters. "If you feel like writing … Or you want to write to me …"

You handed me the notebook. I took it without a word, spun on my heel and started to run. My black ankle boots clacked. I held your gift tight against my chest.

Why did you do that, Jeanne? Why did you give me your ink-blue notebook?

Sitting cross-legged on my bed in my closet-bedroom, I write to you again in the strange notebook you gave me, sturdy with its hard cover and bare, unlined pages. Here I, who never usually write, can make my letters all crooked or even backwards if I want. I can cross out an entire page, I can scribble, glue pictures. I can even talk to you without anyone being the wiser. Not even you, Jeanne.

When you saw me in the library the other day, you noticed how tough I looked in my black boots and dark layers, my silence and sometimes cutting words. But I'm not really like that. No one at school knows me.

Actually, there's something I have to tell you. Last spring, I went with the other grade-nine classes to see a Shakespeare play. Even if I didn't really get the whole story and all its battles, violence, cries and tragic destinies, from the very start I liked the sad prince and his fiancée, who was driven crazy by love and drowned herself in the river. Her name was Ophelia, an incredibly gentle name, don't you think? She looked as though she were asleep on the riverbed, so beautiful with her wet gown clinging to her body and her hair like golden seaweed. Ever since, I've taken her name in secret. You're the first to know.

I went out tonight, my oil pastel buried in my pocket. It's been a long time since I've gone looking for walls and board fences. Night suits the girl in layers. As I've already said, Jeanne, the girl in layers is an alley cat.

Outside, the streetlights threw moon-colored circles on the ground, and I studied the cracks in the sidewalk. They looked like poorly healed wounds. Hands stuffed in the pocket of my hoodie, I walked and walked down darker and darker streets, venturing far beyond my neighborhood.

When I found a wall I liked, a concrete wall, not too rough, I took out my blood-red pastel and did a quick sketch of a heart. I drew a zigzag through the middle. A small broken heart.

I didn't hang around, though, I kept going. You've got to be quick when you're tagging. I had no desire to get caught. From time to time, other broken hearts appeared at my fingertips on new walls, on brick or concrete. I sped up every time another streetlight splashed the asphalt.

A few streets farther down, I stopped short. The road in front of me ended in a cul-de-sac and a torn chain-link fence. Behind it, a long vacant lot faded into darkness. I felt like jumping the fence, just to take a look. But I didn't have a flashlight. I turned and retraced my steps.

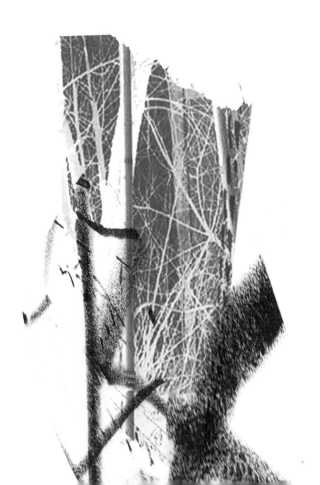

The decibel level in the cafeteria at lunch today is stagger-ing. The fat kid from the library, you know, the one who sent himself postcards, is sitting at a table kitty-corner across from mine, a pile of books stacked in front of him. He reads with total concentration. He doesn't hear the clatter of plates and cutlery, lips slurping, jaws grinding, words piercing ears or the blare from the student radio. He doesn't see kids with trays full of food held out in front of them make their way from the lunch counter to the tables, from the tables to the trash can, then leave.

On the cover of his book, I read *Auto Repair for Dum-mies*. He takes notes, keeps reading, pushes his glasses back on his nose. I hadn't noticed his glasses the other day in the library. I don't even know his name.

He shakes his head like a dog shaking off drops of water, stretches, grabs another book from the pile. An atlas of North America. He lays it flat on the table, opens it. He frowns, follows the curved and tangled lines with his finger. He mutters. Turns the page, once, twice, three

18

times. Smiles. He's happy — he must have found what he was looking for.

I can't handle this school anymore, Jeanne. I can't stand the biology teacher and his frigging questions or the herd of sheep. Earlier by the lockers, doors slammed open and the halls reeked of BO. I don't know how to survive here.

I want … I want to draw big pictures on walls. An image keeps popping into my head of a beautiful naked girl floating in water. Nothing like me, small and dark, distant and close-lipped for the most part until suddenly, without warning, wild rebellious claws and sharp teeth show. No. More like a fish girl.

Oh no! The cafeteria worker just yelled they're closing in five minutes.

The boy looks up, stunned, lost. Back from the beyond. Behind the round glasses, his eyes are a hazy blue. Like they've been bleached.

I think he sees me. He hauls himself up, grabs his stack of books and his backpack. He's leaving. He has a big butt.

Okay. I've gotta go. Cafeteria guy's coming at me with his mop and a threatening look on his face.

I'm scared …
of jumping with a parachute, a paraglider or a bungee
    cord
when there's no emergency EXIT
that no one will ever think I'm beautiful or fall in love
    with me
of taking off all my layers in front of a guy
that no one will hear me cry "Help! Au secours! Socorro!"
of the Vandals who attack anything that crosses their
    path
of failing math
that no one will love me because I'm too different
of discovering I'm a lesbian
of my mom being declared unfit again
of exploding
that you, the writer with the misty eyes, will forget me
of always being invisible
of never knowing my father
of one day meeting my father and him saying, "Yech!
    What an ugly daughter!"
of never doing big drawings on walls

À part ça, ça va.

I work at Dollar Magic every Saturday from nine to five. That was today.

This morning, out back in the warehouse, I threw a white smock on over my clothes and the manager assigned me to a new shipment of boxes. I used the dolly to move the first box to aisle three. "Made in India" written across the top. I slit it open with an exacto knife. You never know what you'll find inside.

I took out a rubber dinosaur. Maybe a brontosaurus. It was brown and green and pretty hideous, with a crest along its back. "Come here, you," I said as I put it on an empty shelf, the one closest to the ground. Kneeling on the floor, I took out another prehistoric beast, then another and another. When I'd finished lining the shelf with rows of well-behaved clones, I went to grab a second cardboard box, this one full of plastic pumpkins. I muttered, "Oh yeah, Halloween's on the way."

What can you buy at Dollar Magic? Small plastic and ceramic objects. Plates from Asia with clumsy designs drawn by children. Fake flowers, notebooks and notepads with kittens or polar bears on the cover. Mugs with maple leaves or fleurs-de-lys. Strawberry, lime and vanilla-scented candles.

Lonely old people walk the aisles, looking for a little something to make them happy — a Christmas angel, a Valentine's Day card, a can of food for a stray cat. Everyone seems lonely in Dollar Magic. And the line-up at the till is long. Cash only.

When I work, lost in boxes, I can't help but think and think, the thoughts swirling and merging, images of lonely people here and starving children in far-off countries who work in the underground economy, dyeing cotton, painting figurines and weaving tablecloths to fill the boxes. I picture all the boxes bobbing over oceans in the holds of ships. Some end up here, at Dollar Magic, to console the abandoned.

Hours later, after more creatures, paper plates, coffee mugs, a voice called out from behind me, "Where's the cat food?" I recognized Delphine, the most beautiful girl in school. "Over there, aisle five." She gave a vague wave. Not a thank-you, nothing. Who gives a damn. Rag girl couldn't care less about the most beautiful girl in school.

Twenty boxes later, right before leaving, I grabbed a mini flashlight and two AA batteries, and stuffed them deep into my jean pocket.

Jeanne, last night on TV, I watched a news report I don't want to talk about! I'll say nothing about it. Nothing!

That's where I saw lost children. One of them sat on a doorstep waiting to be taken to a new foster family. It would be his fifth. His luggage consisted of a green garbage bag with a few clothes inside, his running shoes and maybe a stuffed animal. A little six-year-old boy. His stony eyes stared at the camera. Just once, for a fraction of a second, I glimpsed grief cloud his pupils. I turned off the TV and threw the remote against the wall.

It was too early for graffiti, but I ran outside anyway, tore down streets, left a trail of my broken hearts along an entire length of wall until nothing was left of my pastel stick and the concrete scraped my fist.

Why do people do that to kids? Why? Do you know, writer woman?

The stories you write that I've never read just have to end well, do you hear me? Do you ever think of me? Swear you do!

I just did something strange, like throwing a bottle out to sea. I went up to the student radio station. From there, through the large glass window, there's a bird's-eye view of the cafeteria.

I said, well, mumbled, to the radio crew, "I'd like to be in charge of music once a week from noon till one." They looked down their noses at me, one of them wrote my name down on a kilometer-long waiting list. They're a bunch of snobs. They don't talk to anyone, wear more rings than anyone else and play metal, hip-hop, rap and other rage-filled music. But the guy who wrote down my name was kind of cute — charcoal eyes, bright teeth and a tattoo on the back of his neck.

If I deejayed, I'd play recordings of ocean waves and songs in another language with words no one could understand, but the meaning would be there in its soothing or nostalgic tone. During my first lunch hour picking music, the whole herd would freeze mid-meal, forks suspended in the air, mouths hanging open. The cafeteria transformed into an enchanted forest where time stands still for a hundred years. Every last one of them under the spell of the waves and soothing words.

Maybe I'd leave the studio then, take the stairs, walk up and down the rows of tables. I'd caress a head here, a cheek there, I'd pick up a dropped binder. I would love them. Then I'd return to my ivory tower, and right after the last note of a melody so ancient no one remembers its origin, there'd be a pause, barely long enough to count to three. And bam! They'd all wake up. The regular cafeteria din would return, but more subdued. They'd get up and go to class, where surprised teachers wouldn't have to raise their voices to be heard or shed secret tears. The teachers would wonder, "What in the world is going on?"

The herd of adolescents would have been given a chance to dream, and I'd have lost my urge to come out biting.

But in actual fact, the girl in layers is invisible, and I'm quite sure they'll never give me a shot at the student radio.

Jeanne, something extraordinary happened to me tonight!

I went out again, and this time I took the stolen flashlight along and followed the same path through the streets of the neighborhood and beyond. I brought the ink-blue notebook too, because I don't want anyone else reading what I write to you, Jeanne, especially not my mom. I haven't told you about her yet. I don't really feel like it. I also don't feel like leaving my notebook at school. The Vandals sniff around lockers and pry the doors open with a knife or screwdriver or kick them in. I carry the notebook everywhere with me. Once I reached the cul-de-sac, I snuck through the tear in the chain-link fence.

I turned on my flashlight and started exploring the vacant lot. A path cut across it diagonally. As I followed the path, I saw tires, cement blocks, an old stepladder, beer bottles, mangled bikes, rusted engines — it's like an open-air Dollar Magic. At the other end of the lot, I walked up to an abandoned brick building with large warehouse windows and took a close look at the double doors held together by a lock. I walked around the building, but there was no other door. I did notice a small window at the back, but it was too high to lift myself up onto the sill. I retraced my steps, grabbed the old stepladder, lugged it over easily enough and leaned it up against the wall. From the top rung, I was able to open the window, sit on the sill and sweep my flashlight's beam across the interior. The room looked huge, and the floor didn't seem all that far away.

Without thinking, I dropped inside, forgetting that I could very well stay trapped there forever only to have some archeologist find my skeleton a thousand years from now. "Juvenile female," he'd write in his notes, "still with all her teeth." My notebook made of recycled paper would have turned to dust.

I landed on the concrete floor. My heart raced. I walked slowly through the room, examining the flaking walls. To the right, beside the double doors — how bizarre — I saw the shell of what seemed to be an abandoned vehicle. A bit farther along stood a large wooden table and stool. Plus a rust-stained sink and a dripping faucet.

I took my pastel out of my pocket, headed for the wall at the back and quickly drew my broken heart.

You know what, Jeanne? I think I've found myself a workshop. A secret place I can go to whenever I want, far from others and all the noise they make. At last, I'll be able to do big wall drawings. I've wanted this for so long!

The cops will never arrest me for drawing on these walls. It's not like it's out on the street. And I'll just drag the table under the window and put the stool on top to get out.

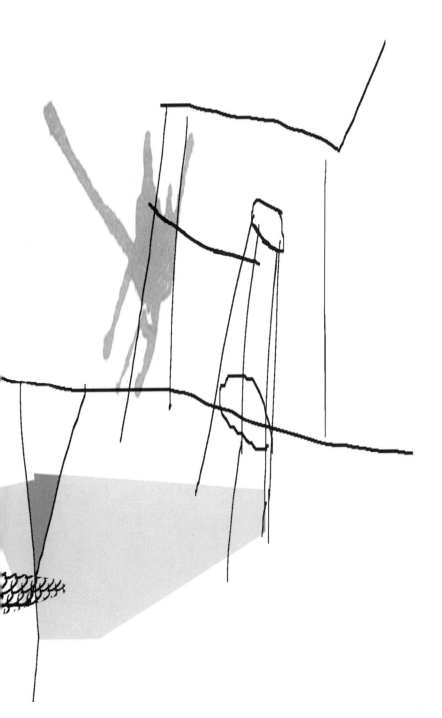

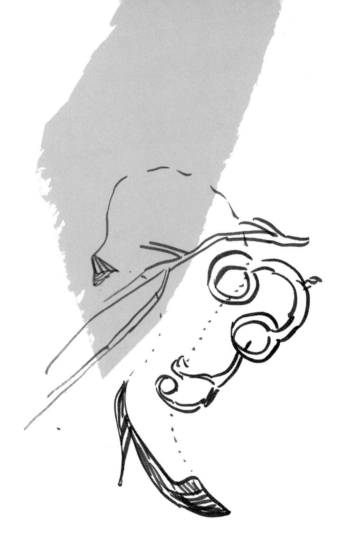

Things are kind of rough at home. My mom and I don't talk very much. "Pass the milk. Pass the ketchup." We try not to make eye contact. Thanks to her work, I'm free to roam the streets and vacant lots at night, to go where I want, when I want. I've got nothing to say about my mom and me. Nothing. A total desert.

Fine. Earlier tonight, around eight, I'm sitting on the turquoise couch in front of the TV, my biology homework on my lap. Perched on top of her stiletto heels, my mom's in a hurry, late, heading for the door. She stops for a micro-second in the doorway looking guilty, thinking, *I know I shouldn't leave my fifteen-year-old teenager home alone five nights a week.*

"Bye, my angel. Get to bed early, you look tired. Don't forget the dishes."

"Bye," I reply, my face expressionless. "Be good, don't yell at your customers, make lots of tips."

She smiles with painted lips, shrugs and shuts the door behind her. I hear her heels clicking down the stairs, then nothing.

So that's that. Family life is simple. Like a play, it's always the same. We pretend everything's okay. Sometimes, not often, she'll meet up with a new lover after work and won't come home until the crack of dawn, bags down to her cheeks.

The night is mine.

I went back to my workshop after school before heading home. I had an hour to myself.

The setting sun shone through the big grid windows. I sat on a stool, my back to the windows, staring at the wall in front of me. It was gray. I held a piece of white chalk in my hand and let the drawing that's been inside me for so long bubble to the surface.

I thought of you, Jeanne. I even imagined you standing there beside me, watching.

Suddenly desire took over, I stood and walked toward the wall.

In no time, I had sketched a naked girl's body, her head upside-down, mouth open, long hair floating. I pulled the stool next to the wall and stood on it for her legs and feet because the girl was life-size. I worked fast in an energy-filled dance as if I'd drawn the girl a hundred times before. As if I knew each line by heart.

I grabbed my bag and the blue notebook, and exited through the window. I left you alone with the first rough outline of my big drawing.

Can you see her? Can you picture her, the upside-down girl, all alone in her aquarium?

In my head, there are …

Salt and vinegar chips. Jalapeño chips. Toasted tomato sandwiches with lettuce and mayonnaise.

A movie of a love story, always the same, that I tell myself at bedtime. The girl is beautiful. A beautiful version of me. The guy is older than she is, but not too much, and rich, but not too much either. He loves her, but she doesn't know it. She walks into the forest alone and trips on a root or falls off a cliff. She's injured her head. He plunges into the forest looking for her, finds her and carries her back. She pretends she's fainted. He whispers words of love, thinking she can't hear him. He kisses her, but she stays limp. He takes her to the hospital and spends the entire night in the emergency room with her, standing next to the stretcher, holding her hand, worrying. In the morning when she wakes, he's gone.

A soft snow-goose down quilt.

A tight black sweater, the boat collar wide enough to show off both shoulders. When I wear it, guys come close and drool like dogs. They don't know about the protective magnetic field surrounding my body, two millimeters out. They'll be electrocuted without mercy.

A journalist who comes across my big drawing on the workshop wall. He talks about it on TV. He uses words like "stunning, daring, brilliant." I don't tell anyone I'm the brilliant artist.

Japanese tourists who take pictures of my tags. They post images of my broken hearts on the Web. All around the world, teenagers print off pictures of my broken hearts and tack them to their bedroom walls.

Sometimes, the guy in my love story looks like the guy from the student radio. The guy with the tattoo on the nape of his neck. I kiss him open-mouthed, but no tongue (I've got to be careful not to think about him too much or I'll blush if I see him for real in the halls).

Catastrophes, like a tsunami breaking over me and carrying me far away, or a nuclear war where I explode into a shower of fire, or a rapist appears and I die. Or smaller catastrophes like a guy walking into the girls' bathroom and peeking under the door just as I'm peeing. Or all the girls in art class busting a gut laughing because they've seen the upside-down girl, and I run far away and can never go back to school.

Claws and fangs.

Ever since school started, most of the kids in art class have wanted to scrapbook and the teacher finally agreed, provided we reinvent how it's done. She wants us to be bold and creative and to make an artist's book. She showed us a few examples.

So for the past two weeks, the class, Delphine first among them, have been decorating special pages to be put together in a book. They keep busy, clucking like hens around the big tables, pinking shears in hand. They glue in pictures of their baby sisters, their favorite celebrities, their cats, and frame them with garlands, stars, glitter, borders, making for pretty illuminated manuscripts. I hate it. I don't know what to do with all that fancy girly stuff. Clearly, there are no guys in our art class.

This morning in class, the two lesbian girls no one talks to seemed unhappy. They mustn't have any nice pictures to glue either. We know they're lesbians because they dared hold hands in the hall and the Vandals called them bitches and pussy-lovers. I don't really like to see girls holding hands — it makes me feel uncomfortable. How can a girl be in love with another girl? At least they're not sheep. Their worried eyes have told me, "We can't be any other way."

In the halls, I see Muslim girls too, with scarves tied under their chins. Something to do with modesty apparently, but I don't like to see girls hiding their hair. As if it was something to be ashamed of. I'm more the never-brushes-her-hair type. There are the hot girls in grade eleven as well, who talk in the bathroom about the guys they hook up with. "He asked me to suck him," says one. "What did it taste like?" asks another. I don't hear the answer. Maybe like disinfectant.

In the end, I spent the hour in class experimenting, mixing all different kinds of blue together. I'm looking for a fluid, changing color for the big drawing in the workshop.

Tonight I visited my upside-down girl carrying a new flashlight I bought at the hardware store. Its light is stronger and shines farther. I took the other one back to Dollar Magic. Seeing the girl in its light, I was disappointed. The other day, I hadn't noticed how stiffly her body lay in the middle of the gray wall. I pictured her more relaxed, almost asleep.

I brought a paintbrush and a water bottle full of my ultramarine-navy blue mixture. I surrounded the girl with color, I want free-floating space for her, weightlessness, where she can dream and be carried away. But the wall drank all the blue. This is more complicated than I thought, Jeanne. Next time, I'll bring a thicker mixture.

As I was getting ready to leave, my eyes settled on the abandoned vehicle by the double doors. I stepped closer. It's quite the vehicle. An old delivery van, snub-nosed. I slid the side door open, the inside looked like a dollhouse. A mini-fridge, mini-cupboards, a gas stove, swivel table, a booth ... I loved it right away.

I even curled up on the booth for a few minutes. I used my backpack for a pillow and fell straight to sleep. Head first into a dream. I was floating just beneath the water's surface and it felt good.

When I woke up, I didn't want to go back to my closet-bedroom for the night. I'd have liked to stay in the calm of the workshop-studio with my chalks, my pastels, my colors, my cans of paint. I'd have eaten tomato sandwiches, drunk bottled water, slept through the night in a three-star sleeping bag.

But it was past midnight and I hurried home, sat on my bed, opened my blue notebook, and like every other time, my fine-tip felt pen started moving on its own, telling you, Jeanne, a bit about my life, my darkness, my hidden desires.

Even though I never slip a single letter into an envelope marked with your name and address and mine in the upper-left corner, I write to you as though you're waiting by your mailbox every morning.

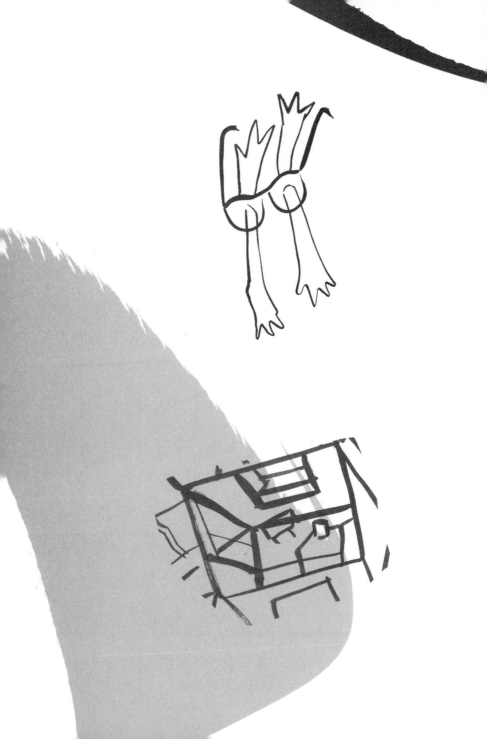

Jeanne, I have some terrible news. Early this morning, before school, I went back to the workshop with a new blue mixture. Once again, I crawled in through the window. I jumped, landed on the table and down to the floor. The sound of the soles of my shoes on the concrete echoed in the large room.

Suddenly, a guy steps out of the dollhouse, a book in his hand! From behind his glasses, two hazy eyes look at me as if I'm a nightmare. The fat guy with the postcards! Unbelievable!

My tough bitch takes over, the one you saw in the library, and I throw my first grenade, "What the hell are you doing here?"

"Did you draw the naked girl?" he asks, as if waking up.

"None of your business, fatso!"

He's instantly red. He looks away, out the window I just clambered through. The knuckles of his fisted hands are white and his voice cracks.

"I squatted here first. Get out."

"I'm staying! This is my art workshop!"

He walks toward me slowly and points to the window. He grabs my arm.

I yank free and yell in his face, "Don't touch me! Don't ever touch me!" I run to the van and start to kick and punch.

He jumps at me, shouts, "Don't touch Caboose!"

I have just enough time to slip into his house, slide the door shut and lock it from the inside. He shakes the handle, his lobster-red face glued to the window.

"Get out!"

"No!"

A screeching silence falls over us. We catch our breath. We don't know what to do, me on the inside, him on the outside. We're surrounded by ruins.

He walks over to the stool and sits down, arms crossed, giving me the evil eye. I half open the window. We eye each other like wary beasts, watchful, lips curled.

"Get out of my spot," he says, barely calmer.

"I don't want you to touch me!"

"No need to worry about that. Rag girls don't interest me."

It's my turn for red cheeks. I grind my teeth. I wait another couple of minutes, but something has to give. Cautiously, I open the sliding door.

I reach into my pocket and pull out my white chalk. I look around the room. My mind made up, I cross to the middle of the workshop and bend over. I draw on the floor, moving quickly. A line divides the space in two.

"This is my side," I say, with a threatening look. "You can do whatever you want on your side. I'm coming on Tuesday and Thursday nights and sometimes before school in the morning. Maybe on Sunday mornings. I'll come in through the back window. I'll never cross onto your side. But I don't want to see your face in here."

The fat guy gets to his feet, stands on his side of the dividing line and replies, his tone matching mine.

"Me neither. I'll come on Monday and Thursday mornings and the other nights. I'll come on Sunday afternoons. Don't go near Caboose. Never call me fatso again."

He goes back into his domain and slams the door. Caboose ... what a name. I stay put, alone and immobile in my territory.

I didn't paint the wall blue, Jeanne. I couldn't do it. It no longer felt like home.

I got back up on my table, then the stool and left.

I'm roaming the streets at night again, drawing broken hearts. They're breaking right apart, I can tell both halves are about to fall. Worse yet, they're breaking into three, the pieces drifting like icebergs, each on its own voyage, one floating off to Labrador, the other following the Gulf Stream and the last, the smallest, melting and vanishing into the sea. Three nights in a row, three oil pastels, but it's not enough. I abandon my upside-down girl, naked and alone in there. Meanwhile, fatso reads his books all cozy in his Caboose, glances at my unfinished girl who's rigid with fear, no water to buoy her up.

At school, I feel as though I'll explode if this keeps up. I feel like breaking chairs and tables, screaming at everyone — the girls with their head scarves, the guys who never look at me, the lesbian girls, the parrot teachers who squawk on and on about math, biology, French, geography, sexuality, history, and use fire-engine red to mark papers, prepare vicious exams, draw alien hieroglyphics on the blackboard, sweat and vent. There's no room left to breathe, anxiety rises, up and up, I draw pieces of hearts, fast and furious, on bits of paper I tear apart, then the sudden urge to destroy passes. No one notices a thing.

How do you survive, Jeanne? Is writing enough to keep you alive? Will my disposable drawings and my hearts scattered over city walls be enough?

Oh, Jeanne! Can I come to your house? Can I break all the locks, sit at your feet, take your hand and place it on my head? Inhale the scent of your perfume? You must have a cat I can pat in your kitchen.

Jeanne, do you hear me crying out your name? Jeanne!

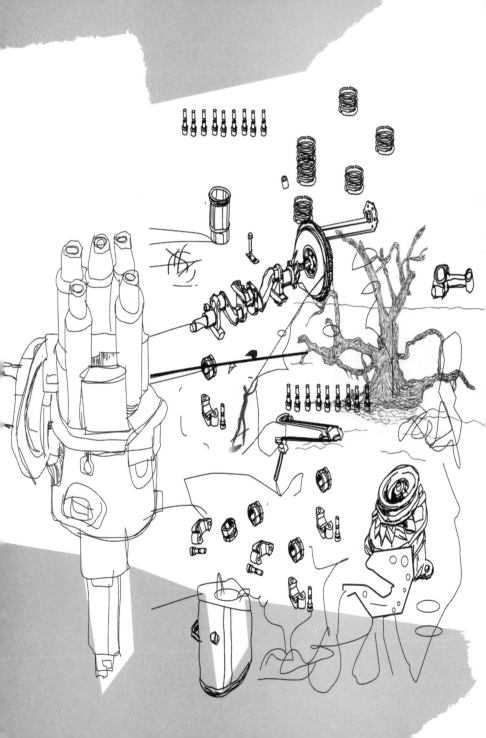

As I walked into the workshop-refuge, I immediately noticed that Caboose was deserted. Walking up to the dividing line without crossing it, I saw all kinds of engine parts laid out on the floor behind the van. There were tools too — a wrench, pliers, a hammer, dirty rags. On Caboose's swivel table, a tidy pile of books waited. On the boundary between the two territories lay three chocolate bars. One milk, one almond and the third, a dark bittersweet chocolate. Did fatso think he could tame me? À la little prince and his fox?

The smell of grease or motor oil floated in the air. I could feel his presence as if he was still here, ogling my naked girl, crossing the boundary, getting close enough to touch her.

I spent a long time studying my upside-down girl, her frightened look, her open mouth and her fingers spread like talons poised to strike. She seemed so alone, a prisoner of the wall, and I could feel her suffering. I knew she wanted to go back to the ocean's depths where no light shines, the only inhabitant a lone, cave-dwelling stonefish.

Still, I tried to keep her here. I caressed her with my fingertips, whispered words of encouragement, but I knew I couldn't bring her to life or take care of her. Not to mention the blue that doesn't buoy her up. I had no idea anymore how to keep her alive.

So I erased my chalk girl with a tissue.

I'm crying as I write, tears pooling on the page, letters melting in the damp, words adrift, just like the girl, broken hearts and the North Atlantic icebergs somewhere between Newfoundland and Greenland.

Jeanne, I can no longer feel your presence.

You've abandoned me.

The year I turned eight, I lived in a foster home. My mom was unfit that year. It was written in her file. I read it upside down on the social worker's desk when she went to the washroom. My mom was away detoxing, but I never knew where. Had I known, I would have raced there and pounded on the door until my knuckles were raw, "I want my mom!"

Before detox, she'd often be sitting at the kitchen table when I came home from school. She separated white powder into piles with a razor blade, weighing them and putting them into little plastic bags. Later, a man in a leather jacket and motorcycle helmet picked up the bags, leaving a few for my mom. Back then, her nostrils were red and she sniffed a lot. Back then, her eyes were feverish and her gestures jerky. When the man in leather arrived, she'd tell me to go to my room and shut the door.

I spent a year with that foster family, they were nice, and we ate shepherd's pie three times a week. There were a number of us lost children sleeping two by two in clean rooms, we didn't talk to each other, we were way too lost.

After her sabbatical year, my mom was fit again.

But by then, I already lived in an impenetrable citadel with a watchtower, a moat and a raised drawbridge.

What's to see down the shopping street on the last Saturday in September during the sidewalk sale? Old people sitting on benches or at picnic tables in front of fast-food restaurants. Moms with strollers, teens dressed like all the other teens, wearing earbuds with wires dangling down their chests. There's a crowd at the sidewalk sale. The mob goes from one store to the next, window-shops, rummages through bins and walks off with huge parcels.

I'm stationed outside, on my feet to keep an eye on Dollar Magic's big tables, inhaling the smell of hot dogs, fries, boiled corn on the cob, and watching little kids walk by with their faces painted like tigers, birds and clowns. I thought I'd be able to create big drawings in the workshop, far from others' eyes, paint water for the upside-down girl, loosen her body, give her freedom to move. But no. Damn fatso.

As I leave, I take a bowl from Dollar Magic that I lodge carefully in my backpack. A hand-painted bowl. Fluid lines in a deep luminous blue ring the outside. Inside there's a pattern of scratch marks in the same cobalt blue. This is the kind of blue I wanted to give the upside-down girl to rest in.

Some bony-fingered child took a lot of care with it in a windowless workshop somewhere in Asia, where he's treated like a slave. It's a gift he's unknowingly given to me. I wonder when I draw red hearts on city walls if I'm unknowingly giving a gift to a stranger?

That night, in my closet-bedroom, I drink hot chocolate from my bowl made in China. I think of the slave child living there and silently give him thanks before taking another sip.

Jeanne! Jeanne! Today after my mom left for work, I saw you on TV. I'm so happy! If you only knew!

The interview had just started, a journalist was introducing you, and it came to me that you're famous. Maybe not as famous as a movie star or a rock singer, but famous for a writer.

At first, you who so loves questions seemed embarrassed about answering hers. Were you worried we might see the real Jeanne? It's because the journalist wasn't asking the right ones. Not like I did that day in the library. Do you remember? Of course, you remember! Not that that's what I set out to do.

Anyway, after a few misses, she asked where you write. That day in the school library, no one thought to ask you that.

"I live in a little house," you answered with a smile, and I could tell you liked the question. "I can hear the faint hum of traffic and children's cries in the schoolyard. I can hear the big heart of the city beating. I need to hear others moving about. Not too loudly — I wouldn't be able to write — but just enough, like a warmth in my veins, a rustling in my ears. My work is solitary. I have a garden out behind my house, by the alley. In the summer, I write under the shade of the weeping birch tree, and in the winter, I work at my table in front of the picture window that looks out over the same garden. That's where I come up with my stories. For the most part, tales of violence and abandonment, tales of butchered love. Yet I do try to write open-ended stories that finish with an element of hope. Hope that needs to be reinvented continually."

Jeanne! You're like me! You need a hidden spot. And your hope is fragile.

The journalist opened her mouth, ready for the next question, but you kept talking.

"I met a young lady in a library a little while ago. I've been worried about her ever since. She asked me why I write and then listened as though the words coming out of my mouth would save her. It troubled me. I'm nothing but a woman who tells stories. But her eyes were so … starved."

That's when I understood you meant me, and my heart almost exploded with joy. You haven't forgotten me! I exist for you! Oh, Jeanne, if you only knew!

"Starved …" repeated the journalist, not understanding a word.

"Yes, you see, she was so hungry, desperate for answers, for love maybe, I don't know. All of a sudden, I wanted to give her something, but what? A thought for the day? A talisman? I gave her a blue notebook I had in my bag."

The journalist tried to change the subject, but you kept going.

"Her name was Ophelia. I'm sure that's not her real name. She took it for herself. Ophelia, Shakespeare's drowned princess, as green as algae drifting just beneath the water's surface. Her body stranded among the reeds. A name no one has dared use for the past four hundred years."

You seemed so sad talking about Shakespeare's Ophelia, and the interview ended abruptly since your airtime was up, and your face disappeared off the screen along with the journalist's — to be replaced by an ad for phosphate-free laundry detergent, followed by another one for some smooth cream that erases wrinkles and cracked skin. I turned off the TV.

Oh, Jeanne! My Jeanne! Don't be sad. I now have proof that you think of me, that you haven't forgotten me. I'm a person to you, and if things get too bad, if I can't take it any longer, I could send you real letters in envelopes addressed to your full name with my return address showing.

But no. When I write to you in secret in my ink-blue notebook, I feel like I can tell you anything that comes to mind. Thoughts too disturbing, too full of claws sometimes to tell anyone for real. This is better.

You guessed right — Ophelia's not my real name. I chose it because Shakespeare's girl floats just like the upside-down girl, who returned to the ocean's depths where she waits, as immobile as a stonefish.

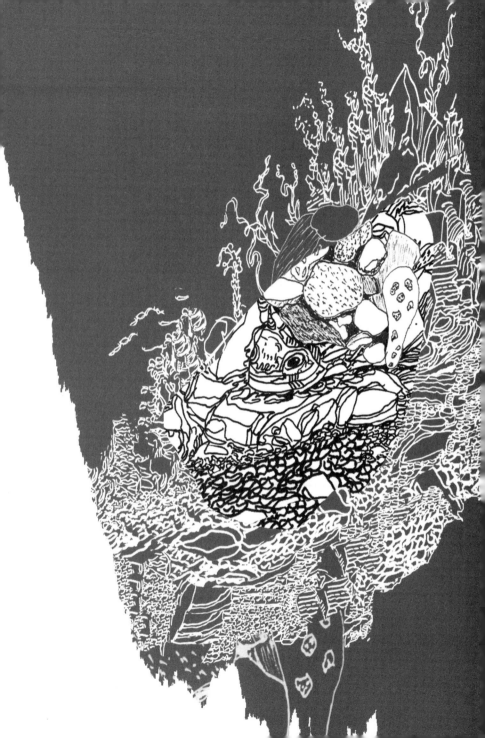

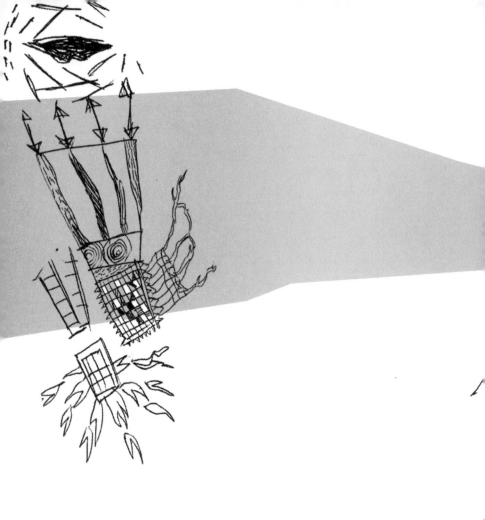

PART TWO
Right-side-up Girl

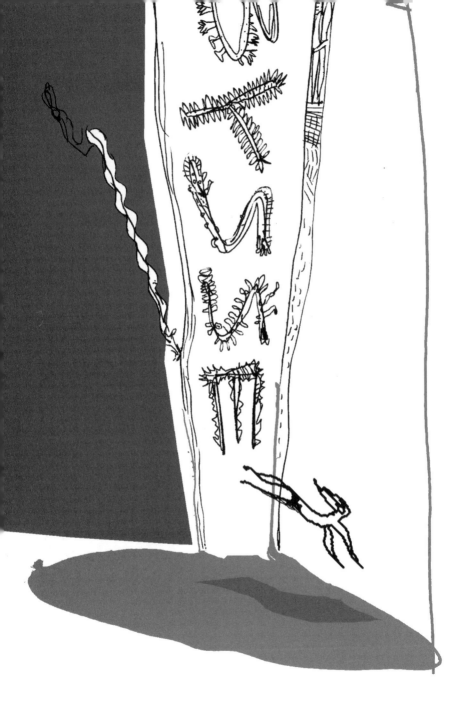

Dear Jeanne,

Since I saw you on TV, my thoughts haven't been as dark or frantic, and I dreamt I visited my upside-down girl in the abyssal kingdom far, far away at the bottom of the ocean. She was floating, safe in the depths, eyes closed. I'm not sure if she felt my presence, but I told her I loved her and would never forget her, then returned to the light.

The day after the interview on TV, I ran to the library and borrowed all of your books. Actually, despite what you might think, I read a lot. What's weird is that it doesn't show at all in French class. My assignments are like rainy days with spelling mistakes sprinkled throughout my nouns and verbs.

I hadn't wanted to read your books for fear I wouldn't like them, but I devoured them all from cover to cover. Your stories are beautiful and moving, Jeanne, and I can see how you don't want your readers to lose heart, how you work hard to envision luminous endings despite all the pitfalls.

But life is full of surprises — things go well or they
don't and we never know why …

a tree snaps in two and falls on your head
the ferry capsizes, you're the sole survivor
a friend becomes an enemy but never vice-versa
a stray bullet pierces your chest
a car heads straight for you and misses
you walk across a landmine

I can tell you worry about all the coincidences that feel
like curses, sudden turbulence, dangerous curves, and you
fight to let life win out in your stories.

One thing is sure, your books don't save me from death.
I would have liked that, but no. Your presence inside me
just might though.

When I woke up this morning, I felt shaky inside. A storm was brewing, and at the heart of the storm an image was growing, ready to spring out of me. I knew I'd go back to the workshop.

At school, I saw fatso in the hallway, and instead of turning away, I attempted a smile. But he stared at the floor and saw nothing. At 10:55, I decided to skip the hated math class by faking a stomachache. The nurse gave me a note, which I just about ripped out of her hand. I fled to the lockers, grabbed my tubes of purple, yellow and orange. Threw the violent, vibrant colors into my bag. No blue. Definitely no blue!

I ran outside, straight to the corner store and bought a liter of red latex paint and another of black. I kept running to the vacant lot and then along the path. I climbed the stepladder, opened the window and landed on the concrete floor.

Then I drop my stuff on the wooden table — paint pots, tubes, paintbrushes big and small, water in a bucket.

On the back wall, facing the double doors, I sketch the outline of a crazy-haired girl with my chalk and draw her larger than life. Her eyes are huge, her mouth slightly cruel, her shoulders as broad as a man's. With my biggest brush, I apply red and black, thick paint splashes all over the floor, like blood, like liquid coal. I dance as I paint. It's a wild, feverish dance accompanied by ferocious cries.

I jump onto the stool and mark up her face, red and black streaks across her cheeks, forehead and chin. With the smallest brush, I paint her lips a dark purple.

The rebel marches. She wears loose red pants and a frayed tunic covered in lightweight black leather armor, like a bulletproof vest. She marches barefoot, weaponless — her strength so great she doesn't need a weapon.

Her jet-black hair is like intertwined snakes pointing east, west and north. She's afraid of nothing and no one. A halo, golden and orange, shimmers around her body.

She marches on and on, and nothing can stop her. I hear her feet pounding the ground. Her mouth open wide, she shouts in her language, "Arghh! Haiya! Ahhhr!" Out of the way!

This is the right-side-up girl.

I wrote the schedules on the workshop walls with a black felt pen so neither one of us forgets, not my roomie, not me. I only see him in French class. I sit at the very back and he sits on the right, halfway down. I bumped into him again in the locker area and looked off into the distance past his shoulder. No one talks to the fat kid with the postcards. I'm sure everyone laughs at him behind his back. I even saw one of the Vandals elbow him in the hall.

The right-side-up girl shines with all her strength from her wall across from the double doors. She's even bigger than I remembered, fiery and fierce. I've brought more bright red paint, graphite pens and a cinnamon bun I eat sitting under the color-spattered wooden table, like a nomad in her tent.

He left a caramel-filled chocolate bar on the chalk line, last night, I guess. Yuck! Caramel's disgusting. He keeps trying to tame me, but I haven't touched any of them, not the milk, not the almond, not even my favorite bar, the dark chocolate one, pure and bittersweet. I'd love to have seen his expression when he opened the double doors and saw my invincible girl staring him down.

Before leaving, I wrote a note that I left on the dividing line next to the chocolate bars. "In here, my name's Ophelia. You?"

Unlike me, the tall fiery girl is not afraid of the outside world. Thanks to her, I feel safe in the workshop and I can write, move freely and paint, even though I share my refuge with a stranger.

I organize my camp. I bring new stuff every trip I make. My blue bowl. A fire-red paint tube, another yellow-ocher one. Paper, library books. A woven rattan mat I found in a garbage can to sit on under the color table. That's where I always sit to eat pastry or chips. From there, I can see the right-side-up girl to my right and the double doors to my left.

When I was little, I'd often sit with my doll under the kitchen table. Mom would let me cover it with a big sheet. The light was softer under there. I could hear my mom moving around, singing along with the radio. She'd sometimes stop and say, "I wonder where my little girl got to …" and I'd whisper, "I'm here, Mommy." It made us both laugh.

Unable to resist any longer, I finally ate the bittersweet chocolate bar. Almost every time since, I've found there on the boundary a new one that I bite into. It's my way of making peace with my roomie. He left me a piece of paper too, with the answer to my question, and I knew right away it was a made-up name because I'd heard his real name in French class as recently as yesterday when our marks were handed out. He got a great mark. All he wrote was "I'm Ulysses" in block letters. In ancient Greece, Ulysses was a great explorer. I wonder if he sent postcards to his wife, who sat waiting at her loom.

I'd love to go back inside Caboose every once in a while to write or chill, but if I want Ulysses to respect the workshop rules, I have to too, right?

I've barely scraped by in three tests this week, and I've gone to the workshop almost every day. Sometimes I do touch-ups to my right-side-up girl, more golden yellow in the halo surrounding her, more jet black in her shock of hair. Most of the time, all I do is dream, protected by the tall fiery girl.

For the scrapbooking project (after all, I do have to hand something in), I brought a stack of white paper and another pile of old magazines and newspapers to the workshop. I chose images at random that spoke to me — no pictures of beautiful girls wearing lipstick, black mascara and pointed shoes, no photos of identically dressed teens, Chihuahuas or guys with massive biceps — but an assortment. I tore the pictures out in no particular order — a little girl balancing bricks on her head, an aqua-blue sea with a smiling dolphin, a man-eating shark, wispy clouds, an iceberg in the shape of a castle, an ancient armless winged statue from a famous European museum, a small brown man and his blowpipe, and lots more, a huge pile of them. I picked the best ones and glued them in, one to a page, torn edges and all. Under the images, I wrote one long sentence that went on from one page to the next. Like a ribbon of words.

This morning, sitting under the color table, I listen to the murmur of the world, I hear the child brick-bearers breathing in Bangladesh, I hear bearded seals blowing through holes in the ice somewhere in Antarctica, I hear the honking of traffic in Jakarta, I feel the ground shaking in the mountains of Asia, I hear the tick-tocking of a suicide bomber's belt, I hear the yowling of cats in the vacant lot, the cracking of ice floes separating from glaciers, the scraping of shells against the ocean floor and the scratching of my pen along the page, I hear water dripping in the workshop sink, this morning I alone am the world.

You too hear billions of hearts beating, Jeanne. Writing that long, never-ending sentence, I felt like you were whispering the words to me and that they flew in all directions, like dandelion seeds on a summer's breeze.

LA NUIT LÀ... LES TRAVAUX, (EPUIS) Y REMALENT
...CES TRANCHÉES, LES... LE BAD,
...CES... CES EXCÈS, LES TICKETS PONT, (LUCK
...PONT, L'HOMME

GROENLAND, TERRE DE FEU, CAP HORN, TERRE-NEUVE, LABRADOR
MAINE, NEW YORK, NEW JERSEY, CAROLINE DU NORD, GÉORGIE
LOIN, PRÈS, LÀ-BAS, ICI, AU LOIN, AU BOUT DU MONDE, À
...CONFINS, JUSTE ICI, TOUT PRÈS
...VENT, À L'AVENTURE

Earlier, on my way out of school, I spotted the guy from the student radio. From overhearing the art girls' gossip, I found out that his name is Samuel. I bet they're all in love with him and will soon glue his picture into their scrapbooks and surround it with pillowy-pink heart stickers. By the way, I didn't bring my artist book to class. The others will just make fun of my pile of torn images glued to the pages linked by that one unending sentence.

I took a deep breath, walked over and without blushing or stammering asked if they'd considered me for the music show. He seemed surprised — obviously not remembering the small dark girl — he half-frowned, then seemed to clue in.

"Oh yeah. The lunch-hour show, right?"

"That's right," I answered.

"Come see me in the studio one of these days. I'll book you a day. Do you have a good selection of CDs?"

"Uh, yeah."

I had no CD selection at all, and my heart twitched like a frantic hare. To avoid blushing in front of him, I spun on my heel and walked away without saying goodbye. I floated just above the asphalt. He's so handsome, Jeanne, if you could only see him — such long, thick black lashes and delicate hands for a boy.

I stationed myself in front of the right-side-up girl as soon as I got to the workshop and asked, "What kind of music would you play? So that Samuel really sees me?"

The corners of her lips lifted slightly in an enigmatic smile. It's like nothing's ever a problem for her.

Yesterday after work, I stopped in at the rummage sale in the basement of the neighborhood church, right across the street from Dollar Magic. I found a sweater big enough for two, a wool hat, a long ruffled skirt and lots of other clothes. I made sure to pick only pale colors and found myself a garbage bag's worth. On my way home, I bought some dye packs.

Today's Sunday and I've come to the workshop early. I dyed my clothes in the big sink and hung them on a long cord strung between the warehouse window ledge and a ring on the opposite wall. It's like hanging your wash out on a laundry line except that everything drips black, red and purple. The sweater big enough for two Ophelias is particularly nice in purple. Same goes for the now dark red ruffled skirt, the lamb's wool hat and the extra-large T-shirt.

I was on a high, Jeanne, with my dyes, my dripping colors, your presence and that of my flamboyant girl, when I heard the double doors slam open.

The fat guy walked in like he owned the place.

I exploded into a thousand raging sparks.

"You have no business being here on a Sunday morning! Didn't you see the schedule?"

"It's my turn. It's noon. You're the one who screwed up."

Then he headed behind his Caboose, where an increasing number of engine parts were strewn across the floor. I ran to look at the schedule. He was right, Jeanne — I'd been so happy in my bubble that I hadn't seen the time go by. You have no idea how frustrated I felt. I started to pick up my stuff, muttering, "Sorry …"

"You can stay. It doesn't bother me."

"No, thanks."

"I like your fresco."

"My what?"

"When artists paint directly on a wall, like Michelangelo or Giotto, it's called a fresco."

This was no normal conversation, Jeanne. First off, he knows some of the great painters of the past. I don't know who Giotto is. I'll have to check him out at the library. But most importantly, he wasn't mad, and I didn't know how to react.

I continued, hesitating, "I'm not an artist. It's just that sometimes I need to do big drawings."

"I don't know anything about auto mechanics. I come here so I can learn on my own."

The situation was becoming more and more bizarre. Here I'd been expecting a war, but I no longer felt angry with this Ulysses. He'd defused my suicide-bomber belt with his chocolate bars and calming voice.

He started hammering away, taking more parts out of his engine and lining them up on the floor. I kept on dunking my clothes in the dye, wringing them out and hanging them up on the line that spanned the length of my territory. We didn't say any more.

Before leaving, curiosity got the better of me and I asked, "What's a caboose?"

"It used to be the last car on a train, where the conductor would sleep."

That first time I saw his Caboose, I thought it looked like a dollhouse on wheels. Now I think it looks like a nomad's caravan.

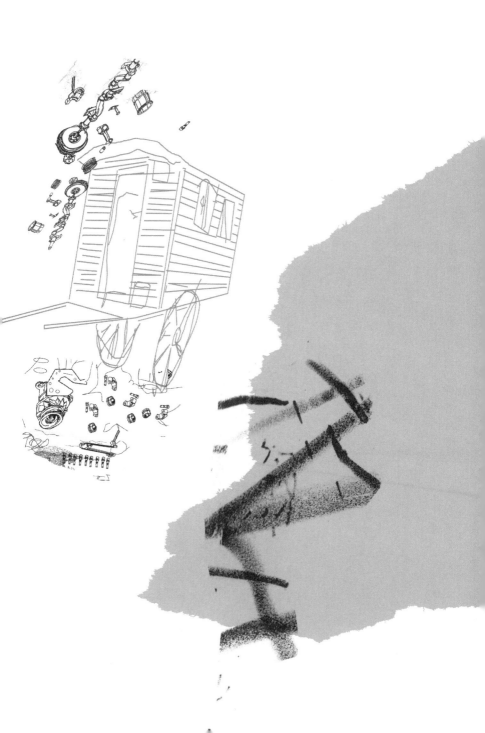

In biology, we learned how to put a condom on a plastic thingy. A guy's erect penis is big and disgusting. The rest of the time, it's limp and hangs between his legs. The girls' giggles rang hollow and the guys pretended none of it was a big deal.

I never want to have sex, Jeanne, that's for sure. Under all my colorful layers, my fabric skin, I don't weigh much more than a feather, I'm as skinny as the bony kids in the desert, I'm ugly too, dark with eyes more full of fear than hatred. Plus … forget it.

Plus, when I was ten, one of my mom's lovers came into my room once, super early in the morning. There, I said it. He used honeyed words, wanting me to take his penis in my hand and then into my mouth. I whispered, "no, no," I started to cry, he didn't have time to push it in me, I bit his hand, roared like a wild animal, my mom ran in, and shrieking, chased him away. We moved soon after that and my mom no longer brings men home.

A good thing I'm never going to send my letters to you, Jeanne.

At dawn, a crazy idea wakes me up. What if I dressed up for Halloween?

I take a good look at all the rummage-sale clothes I'd dyed in the workshop the day I gave up fighting a war because this Ulysses is no warrior, just some fat guy taking his Caboose's engine apart, bit by bit.

I choose a pair of tight pants, a tank top, the dark red skirt, the T-shirt, the sweater big enough for two and a wide belt I cinch around my waist. I tiptoe into my mom's room. She's asleep, curled into a ball, one arm flung over her face, the room stinks of stale cigarettes. I swipe a few trinkets she never wears from her jewelry box, multicolored plastic bracelets, seashell and glass-bead necklaces. Before heading out, I pull the wool hat down to just above my eyebrows.

My jewelry jangles all the way to school, and when I get there, some kids are dressed up and others aren't, just like other years. I get a few vaguely surprised looks of "the rag girl has changed rags" variety, but nothing more. I spend the first hour in the library — Giotto's frescoes are gorgeous, his blue skies so luminous they give me goosebumps — and the second hour in biology. The teacher with the frigging questions asks a whole pack of them — what we think of cloning, in-vitro embryos, surrogate mothers — and not a soul answers, obviously. Suddenly, I raise my hand and my bracelets jingle like bells.

"Yes?" says the teacher, a hint of hope sparking in his eyes.

"All I know is I'd only ever make a baby with someone I loved, not with some unknown man's sperm," I say, turning red.

I'm scared everyone will laugh, but the bell rings shrilly, and we all stand as one, as if programmed that way. The whole herd heads for the cafeteria, and I grab a plate of fries and sit at the emptiest table. What was I thinking, speaking up in front of everyone again? I didn't even use my tough bitch tone. I nibble my fries and stare off into space.

A high-spirited cowboy approaches, laughing, and says, "Give my palm a read?"

At first, I have no idea how to respond, but his voice isn't hostile, we're in Halloween mode, and the others in costume are playing a part, they're not their real selves. In this game, I'm a fortune-teller.

I hesitate for five long seconds, then cautiously take his hand in mine, palm up. I shudder because normally I never touch anyone, and now I can feel a warmth, a weight, as though I were holding a hamster or a hummingbird with quivering wings. I study the strange array of lines and an image pops into my head. "You've just come from a haunted house and you're about to meet up with your frisky horse." Pure nonsense.

He smiles, happy, and turns to the nearby tables. "Hey! Come on over! She reads palms!"

A few people head my way, and I'm so confused — no one ever talks to me at school and now they're lining up, three or four of them, including a one-eyed pirate and a gladiator. I take their hands one after the other, each different in texture, shape and interweaving lines — snake hands, hot hands, sandpaper hands, porcelain hands. I'm dumbfounded.

In the palm of a Vandal dressed up as a big game hunter, I spot barbed wire and say, "I see a square site, guarded, without any shade. On the other side, a desert." I murmur to a girl wearing a headscarf, "A curly-haired child is walking toward you." To Delphine the beautiful, "You live in a skyscraper and from up on high contemplate the city at your feet." To the biology teacher, whose lines continually criss-cross like synapses with their connections and intersections, "Your thoughts travel at the speed of light." He stares at the palm of his hand, as if seeing it for the first time. "Thank you, young sorceress."

People just keep lining up, and I'm in awe of these new hands, always different, always surprising. Joy sparks through me. I sense the presence of others so strongly, yet feel no need to escape. Honestly, Jeanne, this has never happened before.

Finally, after all the hands, smiles and scents, the images fade away. I get to my feet and still dizzy, almost floating, I head up to the student radio where handsome Samuel is in charge of the music. He's not in disguise. He's alone. As he looks for the schedule, I glance out the big window and absentmindedly watch as the students below talk and gesture.

From behind me, Samuel says, "Sometimes I wish everything would just stop down there."

I turn to him. He smiles, showing perfect white teeth, and bends over to look at the schedule. I see his tattoo up close. Three curved lines, one behind the other, in a half-circle. The perfect spot for a kiss.

"What does your tattoo mean?"

"Nothing. So, seems you're a palm reader?"

He stretches his palm out to me, his hand warm and silken, a confusion of lines. My hand trembles slightly. I spot strong lines leading to a narrow valley draped in fog, between mountains as steep as walls. I stammer, "An explorer. A perilous adventure. A forbidden place."

He clamps his hand shut.

"For the music, you can come in December," he says curtly. "The last week of school before Christmas break."

Sometimes my roomie and I cross paths in the workshop. He shows up as I'm leaving. Or vice versa. As long as he leaves me be, I don't mind. The fiery girl is all finished now, there's nothing left to add, and I no longer feel the need to draw on walls like some crazy person. Maybe the right-side-up girl is enough? I have to say, I'm not a real artist. A true painter works day after day, mixing colors, applying them to the canvas. A pianist practices her scales. A ballerina works out at the barre. And you, Jeanne, whether you feel like it or not, you write bits of your novels every morning.

I've gotten into the habit of doing my schoolwork in the workshop. It's better than at home. Ulysses keeps dismantling the innards of his engine, which I doubt he'll ever be able to put back together again. It's none of my business.

Yesterday morning, there was no dark bittersweet chocolate on the dividing line but a book as thick as an encyclopedia with the title *Fresco Art*. It came with a note:

"To successfully paint frescoes, additional tools or an instruction manual are sometimes required." Ulysses had also left a gallon of primer.

I grabbed a scrap of paper and scribbled, "Why?"

Today, an answer was waiting for me, "For that other fresco, the one you erased, you'll need some primer first and then your transparent blue won't disappear into the wall."

I put Mr. Know-It-All's gallon of primer in the corner.

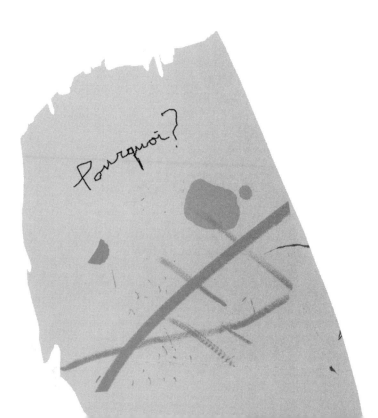

That night, I dreamt I sat in a summer dress in a field surrounded by bright yellow colza. I looked after hundreds of kittens. I protected them and fed them. Then I lay on my back and the little kittens climbed all over me.

It was a weird dream. They walked everywhere, on my belly, my arms, my thighs, my breasts, their paws as light as raindrops. They might even have nibbled my skin with their needle-sharp teeth.

I would actually love to lie outside naked during a summer storm and let raindrops caress me. The wind too. And the wings of monarch butterflies.

Or I could lie on an iceberg and drift south. The sun would beat down, the iceberg would sway, big waves would rock me and make me drowsy.

Do you ever have the same thoughts or dreams, Jeanne? I know you're old, but when you were my age, did you imagine anything similar?

It's starting to get cold. I took an old cloak out of the closet, the inside lined with fur and the outside made of leather, a pair of winter boots and my fingerless gloves. Here in the workshop, I blow on my fingers as I write and draw in the notebook made of recycled paper. Ulysses isn't cold because his polar-bear fat protects him better than any coat could and because he's working so hard to extract the guts of his engine. His puzzle pieces take up a lot of room on the concrete floor.

Today is Sunday, and I stay beyond my scheduled time, even though Ulysses is banging and thumping away, and the smell of motor oil hangs in the air on either side of the dividing line. I've used my fine-tip marker to try to draw random objects lying around, bits of Ulysses' engine, my tubes of color, the blue bowl … My sketches look like they were drawn by a five-year-old.

In the book Ulysses gave me, I spend a long time studying Giotto's and Michelangelo's frescoes, as well as those of cavemen and urban graffiti artists. I do my schoolwork, dream of icebergs breaking off glaciers, traveling north to south and melting as they float on marine currents. I think drowning in the ocean would be a good way to die. I dream of Samuel. Even though I no longer paint frescoes, which kind of makes me sad, I still like coming to the workshop-refuge. It feels like we're in a silky cocoon here.

Earlier, when Ulysses took a break and had a Coke, I asked where he found Caboose.

"Here, the first time I came. The door to the building was locked, but the hinges were so rusted they came right off the doorframe when I pulled on it. When I saw the abandoned van, I adopted it. The place hadn't been lived in for a long time. I have no idea why there's still running water. They must have forgotten about it when they left. I think it used to be a warehouse."

Phew. He just strung seven sentences together. Ulysses, talkative? It makes me want to continue the conversation.

"Don't you think it's kind of funny that the two of us were looking for a refuge at the same time …"

"Yeah. I wanted a place to dream of traveling, pore over atlases, read stories of the great explorers, learn. I like learning on my own."

"Why are you taking the engine apart?"

"To find out what's not working. And rebuild it again afterwards."

He hasn't understood my question. I try again.

"But then what? What are you going to do with a rebuilt engine?"

"Leave. I'm going to leave with Caboose once I turn eighteen."

"Where to?"

"I'll head south, so far that it'll turn cold again. Toward Patagonia, Cape Horn. I want to cross both the Americas. Visit every country."

"That'll take a while …"

"Two years."

"Are there icebergs off Cape Horn?"

Mr. Know-It-All frowns, thinking. "Newfoundland's good for icebergs. And it's closer to home. You interested?"

"Nah. I was just wondering."

He goes back to tinkering. A bit later, he wipes his cheek with his hand, leaving a trace of grease behind. I can't help thinking it'll take him a thousand years, and since he's a terrible mechanic, even then he won't be able to start the engine. And if Caboose doesn't belong to him, he won't be able to drive it to Cape Horn. Where will he find the money to pay for two years' worth of gas and grub? Ulysses is a pretty stupid dreamer.

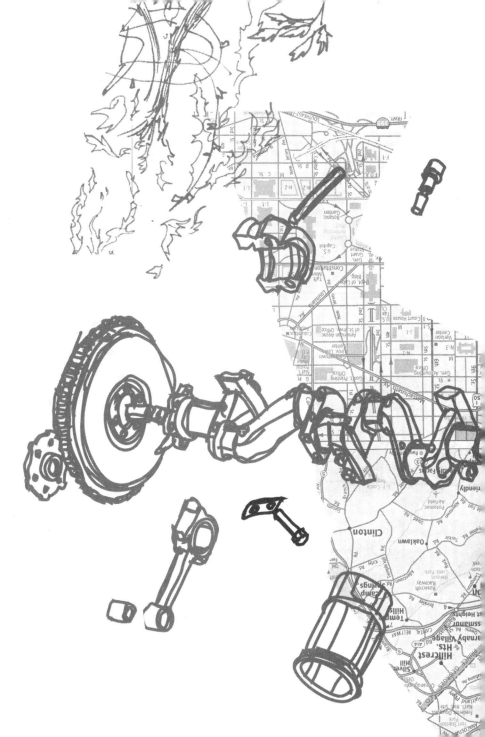

Dear Jeanne, it's midnight. I'm not asleep.

I know you'll never read my letters locked away in the ink-blue notebook stuffed into my backpack.

But when you're on the verge of drowning, it's imperative to find some kind of wreckage, an uprooted tree lying on its side, an object floating on the surface of the raging sea to grab hold of. You're my life preserver — I chose you for that purpose and won't change my mind because it's too discouraging to dwell on the fact that I'm talking-writing to someone who has no idea I've been sharing my secret, incomprehensible life, the one I'm ashamed of, with her. So because you looked at me once, just once, as if I was someone important in your eyes, I'm able to continue on the tortuous path that is my life. And that's that.

When you're the daughter of an unfit mother who's back to being fit but could revert to unfit at any time, when you're the daughter of a chain-smoker who's bound to die of lung cancer just like it says in fluorescent letters on cigarette packs, of a woman who's willing to sleep with any man wearing cowboy boots, and of an ex-coke sniffer, as you can imagine, Jeanne, the choice of life preservers is pretty limited, and so you grab onto whatever comes your way. And if the person who happens along is you, the writer, you who took an interest in the girl in layers, with concern and something close to love in your eyes, who dug through your bag, brandished the momentous and wondrous object I now write-scribble-draw-think-allow my rage and loneliness to surface in — thankfully it's thick and will last a good long while — then that life preserver is to be cherished, clutched tight, never to be let go. Told everything.

Like tonight, the worst part is the heat in my belly whenever I think of him, the guy with the tattoo whose name caresses the inside of my mouth like honeyed milk, Samuel Samuel Samuel. What to do?

I wish you a good night, Jeanne, my one and only Jeanne, my soft buoy, my goose down pillow.

The bell rings, the horde spills into the halls, heads for the exit. I hurry with the others when suddenly I spot him. Without thinking, with no plan of any kind, I follow him, zigzagging through the halls toward the exit. I pass the art teacher and she grabs me by the arm.

"You haven't handed in your scrapbooking project. Did you forget?" she asks.

I mumble that I'd tried something different, taken risks the way she'd asked us to, but that it didn't work out, I'm starting over and will bring it in for next class, promise, then run to catch up to him. Where did he go? I run and run, but I've lost him, I want to see him, his beauty, his lashes too long for a boy, his wool toque pulled down to his eyes, his long stride, and I run, right past two Vandals and their fists, I run but he's disappeared, no, I spot him, already outside, walking with big springy steps.

I scurry behind and follow him through the neighborhood streets. I picture the tattoo under his wool scarf, I want one too in the same place, I'll go to the tattoo parlor, I'll mark the kissable spot with a bird's wing, a crescent moon, a sprig of forget-me-nots. It's cold, a bitter wind from the north, and small dry snowflakes slap my cheeks. I keep my distance. He walks with his hands in his pockets and his head tucked into his shoulders. Lost in his thoughts, his dreams. So far from Ophelia.

He enters a house, his, but do I know that? I wait on the sidewalk across the street for him to emerge, like a dog waiting for its master. I hurt. Love hurts, right in the gut. I hurt all over. Have you ever felt like this, Jeanne? Am I normal? Isn't love supposed to make you happy?

Not me.

Not my mom either, I don't think. She's always changing lovers — happiness eludes her.

I stay put on my side of the street, hopping from one foot to the other, toes frozen and fingers curled in my mittens. Me a risk-taker? When would that have been?

A bit later, I leave. I'm too cold.

Sunday again. My roomie came to the workshop early this morning. "I'll leave if you want me to," he stammered, but his presence doesn't really bother me anymore, I just grumbled out of habit. We never go into each other's territory, that's sacred space, and it's because we respect the dividing line and keep quiet that we can both stay here in this place with no adults, no school, no noise made by others.

Ulysses is happy because he discovered, just yesterday, that the electricity works — I don't really know how. He opened the breaker panel and all he had to do was lift the lever. Today he showed up with a space heater and two clamp lamps that we set up, one on my side and one on his. Now we can stay longer, even at night, if we want to. The heater's set up on the dividing line, and we have to work closer together in order to feel its warmth. I'm starting to wonder whether Ulysses might be rich. I know he bought the fresco book in a thrift store — he told me so the other day. Or maybe he steals things too. Sometimes I don't find him quite as stupid or as fat. It's weird, like we could maybe become friends one day.

As for me, I practice drawing objects from the workshop, others I find in the vacant lot and more still that I borrow from Dollar Magic, then return the following Saturday. All these clumsy drawings are a bit lame, but I need an excuse to keep coming, right?

Sometimes I feel a sadness surfacing, as if something is missing. In those moments, I envy Ulysses who never wonders about tearing his engine apart in the hope he'll be able to put it back together again. I chase away any sadness with my funny-looking felt-marker sketches in the notebook.

In any case, today I've brought a big bag of jalapeño chips that I set down in the heater zone. We take turns reaching in.

With his mouth full, Ulysses asks what in the world I'm doing in the notebook that follows me everywhere.

"I scribble."

"What do you scribble?"

"Letters."

"You won't be able to send your letters if you write them in a notebook. Unless you rip out the pages?"

"They're not for sending."

"What's the point of writing a letter if there's no recipient?"

He's getting on my nerves. Who says "recipient" anyway?

"I feel like writing to someone."

"So … is this an imaginary person?"

"No, she exists."

"So then, send her your letters."

"I'd rather not."

"You could do what I did with the postcards."

"No way! You sent them to yourself, like a cat chasing its tail."

"I didn't have anyone to write to. You do."

"Leave me alone!"

We went back to our pursuits. A scribble here. A hammer strike there. Two mutes who've got nothing to say to each other. Then an hour later, a question comes to me, burning my tongue, and I ask it.

"Do you like girls or guys?"

"Girls."

"I like guys."

The silence stretches out, and I add, "I've never had sex."

"Me neither."

Silence.

"Is there a particular girl at school you like?"

He seems surprised, hesitates, then a pained expression washes over his eyes. He shakes his head.

"No …"

"There's a guy I like. He's handsome. But I don't dare talk to him."

A thousand silences.

"I'm fat," whispers Ulysses, his head bent over the scattered engine parts. "You called me fatso, remember?"

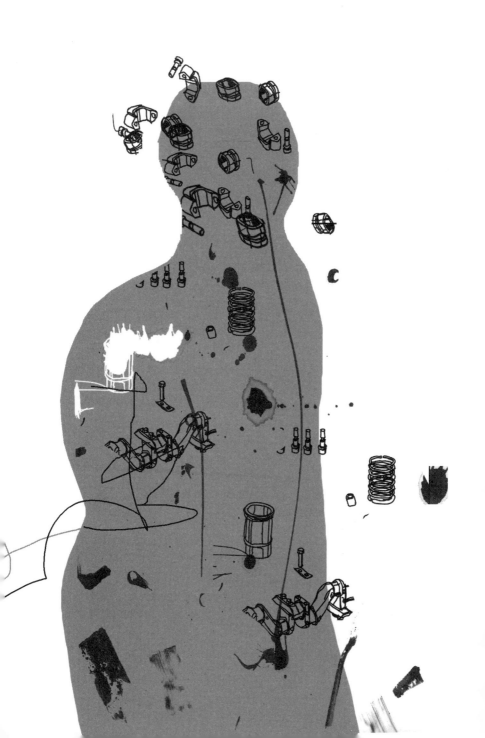

I wavered, then ended up taking it. A small plaster Buddha. It reminds me of Ulysses. A way of asking for forgiveness. I swear it'll be the last time I steal from Dollar Magic.

What do you think, Jeanne? Should I stop?

I like to steal. When I slide an object into my pocket, I feel, I don't know ... powerful. I feel like I'm pulling one over on my boss, who pays me under the table like some child slave in Asia. I steal to give myself little presents and because the future resembles a dead bird. My grades at school are so low, I'm going to fail, I'm not good at anything, my drawings make no sense (I did end up handing in my hundred pages with a hundred torn images of the world and my unending sentence to my art teacher whose eyes opened wide in astonishment).

Stealing is exciting.

Stealing is as dangerous as drawing broken hearts on walls by night.

Stealing is banishing all the Delphines of the world into one corner.

Okay, I'm going to stop. Promise. I used to think I was entitled. I've been stealing since the year of the unfit mother. I hid my treasures in my backpack, bits of crayons and erasers, a pen. Since I found the workshop and since Ulysses and I have been talking instead of hurling insults, I don't feel like it as much.

When I dropped by the workshop this morning, I left the little plaster Buddha on the chalk line.

It's weird. Ulysses and I pretend not to know each other at school, and yet without ever saying a word, we have a standing date at the workshop every Sunday. He brings dark bittersweet chocolate, I bring my famous bag of jalapeño chips, and we share. The floor is now covered in all the bits he managed to pull out of Caboose's entrails, which he examines, auto repair book in hand, looking worried. He'll never be able to put them all back together.

I know nothing about him. I sometimes want to ask questions like "Do you have sisters, brothers, parents? Tell me!" but quickly change my mind. There are too many things I don't like about him. For starters, he's too fat. Then there's the fact that they say a Vandal made fun of him in the locker area again, called him a glasses-wearing nerd, and he didn't defend himself. Plus, he doesn't see the me that exists under all these layers. We can't say we're friends.

At any rate, we're together in the workshop today. I open the gallon of white primer and stir the paint with a stick. I've decided to paint the north wall, the one across from the grid windows, where I traced the outline of my upside-down girl. I'm going to paint the wall right up to the dividing line.

"You going to repaint your fresco?" he asks, looking up from his manual.

"No. The light looks better on a clean white wall than on a bare concrete one."

He turns back to his reading, seated among his dismantled engine parts. He looks like the plaster Buddha. He hasn't said a word about it. Maybe he doesn't like it? Oh well. I start applying the white with a roller. The thick paint penetrates the concrete, the wall brightens up. My right-side-up girl smiles from the back wall. Time passes.

Suddenly, Ulysses stands and walks toward the chalk line.

"I'd like to have a dog in the workshop. He could spend nights here, like a guard dog, and you and I could take him for walks in the vacant lot whenever we're here. I'll pay for the food."

I start to laugh.

"Hard to get a dog out through the window!"

"You could just go out the door with him."

"Cross your territory? Never. Then you'd want to come into mine!"

"I won't! You'd only walk through with the dog once a day, that's all. I give you permission."

"I'll think about it."

"I'd like a sheep-herding dog," adds Ulysses, "because I'm going to raise sheep later on after my travels. Or be a vet."

I don't respond. But I do think it's a good career choice. Better than a rock singer or lawyer. Or cell phone salesman.

I'd happily live surrounded by trees and fields with tons of kittens. Or in a place like this, a place to paint, draw, write in. Or both. But that's not a career. I still don't know what I'll do later, when it's time to be grown-up and responsible, with nothing around anymore but old folks and almost no kids. Maybe our drinking water will have run out too. Maybe I won't become anything at all. At school, we have to decide now for later. Physics and chemistry for future scientists. French for future writers. And so on.

Ulysses is big. He must weigh in at ninety kilos with his Buddha fat and his too-long arms. Arms like that could wrap three times around a skeletal girl. A boa constrictor suffocating its prey.

He takes off his glasses to talk about his dream guard dog some more. I realize his eyes are the same blue as a transparent sea.

It would be great if he could convert his fat to muscle.

In the cafeteria, Samuel sat at my table, actually there wasn't really any room elsewhere. He put down his tray, gave me a nod and a quick glance, something like curiosity shining in his eyes behind his curly lashes.

I felt myself start to blush. First my throat, then my neck, cheeks, forehead. I was so hot. He saw it spread right to my hairline, an awful color that everyone could see. I was so embarrassed, but I couldn't stop the red tide. Had he figured out that I'd followed him last week?

Samuel looked concerned. "What's wrong? Are you running a fever?"

I shook my head from side to side. No words could get past the lump in my throat. I wanted to disappear. All the kids in the cafeteria could see I'd turned into a peony because of him. I stared at my plate and tried not to cry with the shame of it.

He ended up walking off because another spot opened up and I just looked too ridiculous. Rag girl's fallen for the handsome Samuel? What an idiot!

Delphine, sitting a bit farther down, got up and grabbed her tray. As she passed my table, she hissed between her teeth, "Don't touch."

The room slowly emptied. I left too, my head down.

I never blush when Ulysses looks at me, except when I'm angry.

But Samuel's eyes are electric. He electrocuted me.

What is love?

Is it when Samuel stares at me, when my body goes berserk and my legs collapse?

Or is it when I pat a cat in the street and my heart drowns in tenderness?

Is it when a guy looks at a girl with phosphorescent eyes?

Is it when a guy looks at a guy that same way? A girl at a girl? An old man at a young girl?

Where does love start? In the gut?

How long does love last? A second? A lifetime and beyond?

I don't love anyone for real, Jeanne. If I dive down, down to my very depths, all I find is dark and hard. Nothing alive.

Jeanne, I was walking toward the workshop-refuge after school as night fell. Then I get to the chain-link fence around the vacant lot and hear steps. I turn. A shadow stops. The streetlamp's too far away. I can't see his face. What if it's a Vandal? They wreaked havoc in the locker area this week. The police came. The principal spoke over the intercom. "We deplore. Blahblahblah. We will severely punish any acts of vandalism. Blahblahblah. We are taking measures to protect our school." Who is he kidding? Drug dealers come right up to the doors on Friday afternoons! Nothing's easier than buying their crap.

I climb through the fence. The shadow stays on the other side, watching me. It's four in the afternoon, I'm not afraid of the dark, but I start to shake. I race across the vacant lot, shivers running down my spine, and enter through my window. Ulysses is there, sitting on the floor with his engine bits spread out around him, looking miserable. That gets to me.

"When are you ever going to rebuild your engine? Huh? When? Do you have any backbone whatsoever? A Vandal followed me here."

The color drains from his face.

"Janvier's coming next week to help me with the engine," he stammers.

I don't know who Janvier is. I don't care. I don't care

about Ulysses, that wimp. I cross the dividing line, rummage through his tools, grab bits of wooden planks left lying around. I go back to my side, hammer in hand, climb on my color table.

"What are you doing?"

"I'm barricading the window!"

"How will you get in?"

"I'll go through your side. I'm scared!"

I feel like crying, and my high-pitched voice, my trembling hand holding the hammer give me away.

For a moment, Ulysses watches me from behind his glasses, then he gets up, crosses the boundary with a heavy step and takes the hammer from my hand. He climbs up to my spot on the color table, setting off all kinds of creaking and groaning, and starts hammering nails. Ten blows and the work is done. The window is condemned. He goes back to his side, pokes around in Caboose and comes out with something cradled in his palm.

"Here. It's the key to the lock."

I'm speechless. Everything happened so fast.

"Draw me," he says.

"What?"

"Draw me on the wall, like her. Wearing armor."

Jeanne, I had no idea what he was talking about.

"Your fresco. The strong girl. Draw me as a warrior."

"Where?"

"Next to her!"

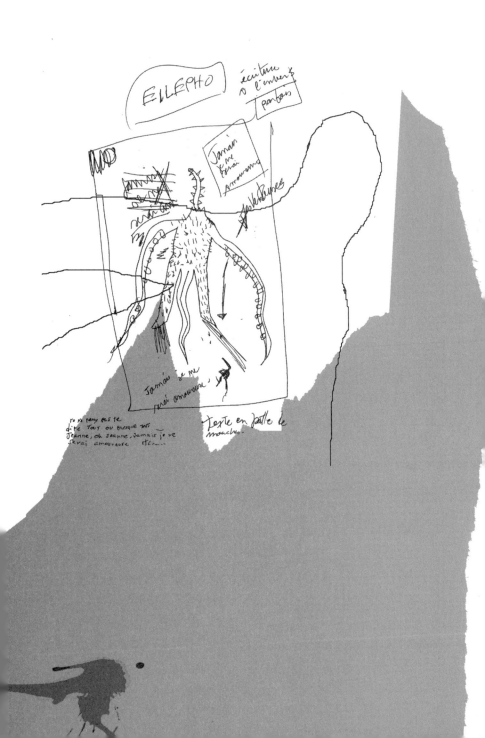

Dear Jeanne, I'm too excited to sleep!

Today Ulysses asked me to paint him on the wall next to the right-side-up girl, like a couple of warriors. At first, I didn't think I could do it.

"I don't know how to draw the outline of a man's body. I can do a girl's body because I feel it from the inside, but you ... no. I don't even know how to draw or paint, don't you get it?"

"I'll stand against the back wall. You can trace my outline with a pencil, chalk, whatever you want. Then you can paint my face and warrior gear, like you did for her ..."

"No."

He crossed the dividing line, walked up to the tall fiery girl. He took off his glasses. Back against the wall, arms slightly raised, eyes imploring, he whispered, "Try. I need this."

I took pity on him. I grabbed a pencil from the color table.

"Shift to the left some. Raise your arms higher. You're too low. We won't see your feet."

"Hand me *Fresco Art*."

He stepped onto the book. He was bigger than the fiery girl. I didn't know where to start. I snagged the stool. I let the tip of my pencil glide around his left shoulder. His face was close to mine. I saw his ocean-blue iris. I saw his Buddha-like chubby cheek. I felt his breath against my neck. He smelled of ferns. I traced his giant body, his too-long arms, his solid thighs. I was shaking. Too close, Jeanne. Do you understand? What if he exploded, trapped me in his tentacle arms? You never know what they're capable of.

When I was done tracing him, breathing in his scent in spite of myself, he pointed both clamp lamps at the back wall. I asked him to go inside Caboose and not look my way. I didn't want him to see me in the frenzy of jumping and dancing as I painted. Without a word, he disappeared into his caravan.

"Close the door!"

I gathered my paintbrushes and my remaining colors together. Standing before the outline of Ulysses' body, I waited, immobile.

All of a sudden, I threw myself into a wild dance. I painted fast, color splashed onto his body, his armor a golden yellow, blue for the war paint on his face and his eyes, his hands big, his feet solid, as fierce as the right-side-up girl. But even stronger, thanks to his muscles. Boys have more muscle, their bodies are harder. When I was done, I thought they looked like brother and sister, standing side by side.

I cried out, "Ulysses! Come see!"

He stepped out of Caboose. He walked up to the dividing line.

"Those Vandals better watch out," he said.

We started to laugh. Fear beat a retreat.

This morning by the lockers, Ulysses screwed up the courage to speak to me, trying not to move his lips, hoping no one would notice.

"Did you see on the news last night about the dogs from the illegal kennel?"

"Yeah."

"Meet at the SPCA at four, okay?"

I nodded and we headed off in separate directions through the crowded hallway.

It was awful, the dogs they found there. The newscaster explained how they were starving, living in their own excrement and how bad it smelled. "Most will need to be euthanized, but a few will be put up for adoption." The poor creatures appeared on screen, filthy, shit clinging to their fur, skin and bones, crazy-eyed.

So I show up at the SPCA right at four. Ulysses is already there waiting for me in an old worn-out leather jacket I've never seen before that makes him look like a thug. We step up to the reception desk and ask to adopt one of the abused dogs. The employee informs us that the dogs from the illegal kennel are damaged, don't know how to behave like dogs, panic at the slightest noise, relieve themselves anywhere and everywhere, can't identify friendly humans, and really they need special foster families, experienced masters who can train and care for them. At any rate, we're not old enough. He doesn't add that we look homeless ourselves, especially me, disheveled with a ratty cloak, but the disdain in his eyes betrays him. I know exactly what he's thinking.

"So there's no way you could adopt one of those dogs," he concludes, as stiff and polite as a cop.

"Screw that!" Ulysses says to his face. "We're the best choice because we're just like them, don't you get it?"

We turn our backs. Head for the door. I can't believe it. Did Ulysses really just yell at an SPCA employee?

The man runs after us. We think he's going to chew us out because we weren't all nice and polite.

"Listen, I've got one here in the back who's going to be euthanized this afternoon. He has nothing to lose, maybe he'll be happy on the streets with you two."

"We don't live on the streets," grumbles Ulysses. "We have families, a single parent for her and a blended family for me, just like everyone else. I bet you're divorced. And we go to school."

The shelter employee shrugs. This time I'm sure he'll kick us out for impertinence, but no. "He's a good dog.

Come see." It hits me that the idea of killing this particular dog hurts him.

Oh, Jeanne, the dog looks like Ulysses' dream of a sheep-herding dog. Black-and-white and intelligent-seeming, one ear up, the other folded over. He pushes his muzzle through the bars of his cage and gives us a gentle look. I offer my hand. He licks it.

"An accident," says the employee. "We operated but no one wants to adopt a pet with three legs instead of four. He's had his shots, he's healthy. Do you want him?"

We take him right away and leave. Happy to have saved a dog from death.

As we walk to the workshop-refuge, I ask, "So, you have a blended family?"

"Yup," grumbles my roomie. "It's not great."

"How did you guess I live with a single parent?"

"I didn't, I made it up!" he answers, laughing.

We reach the vacant lot. Ulysses throws a stick, the dog jumps into the air and lands on all three legs, the stick in his mouth. "Come, Tripod. Good dog." He's just found a name for him.

Ulysses is playing with Tripod as I write. It's funny. Earlier, when he told off the attendant, it was like I saw him lose a kilogram.

You know what, Jeanne? The warrior I painted on the wall is working!

In the girls' bathroom, Delphine says to Sarah Maude, loud enough for me to hear, "Guess what? Rag girl's in love …"

"With who?" the other one laughs.

"You should have seen her when Samuel sat down across from her in the cafeteria. Her hair all over the place, her eyes popping out of her head! She choked on a mouthful of macaroni!"

"Oh no! Not Samuel!"

The girls laughed and cackled away. I wanted the floor to open up and swallow me.

But I did something I'd never done before. I walked up to them and barked, "You're just jealous because he never talks to you. NE-VER!"

Jeanne, I'm so ashamed. Before school's out, everyone will know I'm in love with Samuel. It was my secret. He's going to kill himself laughing when he hears about it, and if he makes fun of me, I'll die for sure!

Ever since that time in the cafeteria, I've been careful not to cross paths with him in the hall anymore. I walk with my head down. I graze the walls. Thankfully, we have no classes together. I'll never go back to the student radio station.

Sitting on the floor in front of the dividing line with Tripod on my lap, I listen to Ulysses talk about his travel plans. Until he turns eighteen, he keeps busy working on his itinerary.

He unfolds his first map and sets it on the chalk line.

"I'm going to leave at the start of winter and take the highway so I'll go faster the first day. As long as it's still cold out, I won't be able to sleep in Caboose. I'll head down to the American border and show them my brand-new passport. 'Where are you going, sir?' New York, I'll tell the border guard. 'How long?' For Christmas. Visiting friends."

I burst out laughing. His Quebec accent in English is pretty bad. No one's going to understand him.

"Why would you lie to the border guard?"

"If I say I'm going all the way to Tierra del Fuego, they'll ask me tons of questions. Everyone goes to New York."

Ulysses is a planner. He's thought of every last detail for his trip. Personally, I think he's too organized.

"Look at my atlas. I've decided what route to take to get there."

I see a muddle of red, blue and green lines on the map and points connecting them, the names of cities, rivers and mountains. He slides his finger along the route and keeps talking, undaunted. He recites names and numbers — Interstate 80, Adirondacks, Savannah. He's map-traveling. His trip has no smells, shapes or sounds. It's nothing like reading the lines on the palm of someone's hand, feeling its warmth and weight. It's boring as hell. I interrupt.

"Ulysses, stop! I don't care about that stuff! I can't see anything! MAKE ME SEE IT!"

He slams his atlas shut. Closes his eyes to better focus.

"I'm at the wheel," he says, and his voice drops, deeper, weightier. "I cross the States from North to South. I listen to the blues for the drive, like truckers do. By the second day, it's getting hot and I drive with the window down. I pick up a pretty girl hitchhiking. We go to the seaside, I kiss her. After, I continue on my way."

That's his trip? Meeting girls in miniskirts with belly-button rings, thong panties and painted toenails? What an idiot! Just like all the other guys. A beautiful girl in the sun. I hiss like a snake, "You're too fat. No girl will go near you."

His face flushes, he growls, "I'm sure that under all those rags, you've got no breasts, no hips, no butt! I bet there's nothing but bones under there!"

We stay put, stare each other down, rage spilling out our nostrils. Face to face, separated by a chalk-drawn line. I jump to my feet. Tripod flees, his tail tucked between his legs.

"You can't even put your engine back together. Your big plan is nothing but hot air. It'll never happen!"

"All the guys at school think you're hideous! You can bet no one wants to kiss you!"

Tripod whimpers and races back and forth from one to the other. I hide out under the color table, I cry, the right-side-up girl and the warrior look sadly at each other, Ulysses kicks at his engine parts. Tripod plops down on the dividing line, whimpering like a lost puppy.

I look up. The right-side-up girl stares into my eyes. "A fight isn't the end of the world. You can glue the pieces back together. Try."

I've gone back to living under the color table, which I've covered with a blue sheet. That's where I draw and write now. In my nomad tent, the light is tinged with blue. I live at the bottom of the sea. All that's missing are the sand and stonefish. Sometimes Tripod joins me.

Up above, the two warriors are yawning their heads off, their eyelids heavy with boredom. This morning Ulysses is already here, sitting at the swivel table in Caboose. He doesn't work with his hands anymore, just deciphers maps, atlases, travel guides. But how will he travel if he doesn't rebuild his engine? If he doesn't take any driving lessons? If he dreams and does nothing else? We don't talk anymore. The fences aren't mended between us.

Jeanne, what will become of me? Why do I have to destroy everything? Why does it all come back to me like a boomerang? Why am I such a monster?

Sometimes I want to stake out your front door and wait for you to step out. I'd run over and say, "It's me, Ophelia! Do you recognize me? Please give me a hug."

Or I'd head for the back alley and peer through the loose planks in the fence.

But that's impossible. Whenever I close my eyes and picture your garden, I clearly see it surrounded by brick walls. The only access is through the house. Streetside, your house is locked tight with maximum security bolts and sliding chains. You never show anyone your garden.

I used to be so proud of having painted the right-side-up girl and her companion with the war paint on his face, but now I only come to the workshop to see Tripod and hide out in my tent. No images come to me. I only draw in my notebook to practice.

"Tripod! Come here, boy!"

He runs to my blue refuge, licks my face. His tail wags all over the place. I see his love for me shining in his eyes. I bury my nose in his fur.

"Tripod! Come!"

He runs over to Caboose, launches himself eagerly at Ulysses.

"Here!"

"No! Here!"

Tripod runs from one to the other. We're driving him crazy.

Delphine, being beautiful on the outside doesn't mean you're beautiful on the inside. I've seen your spitefulness.

Samuel, who are you really? An angel? An alien?

Ulysses, I'll have you know that under your baby Buddha fat, you're so, so skinny, as skinny as me.

You, Vandals, as you walk down the halls two by two, your hands balled into fists, a sneer on your lips, I picture the switchblades in your pockets, I want you dead and buried in a common grave thousands of kilometers from here.

You, my Jeanne, your thoughts are with your garden plants, sleeping through the winter under the snow. And because they're in your thoughts, they don't die in their sleep.

Me, under my layers, my skin, my muscles, my entrails, as far as can possibly be imagined, lies a stone. A stone that loves no one.

Tripod, your tongue licks that stone. My stone becomes a marshmallow.

And you, art teacher, why did you pin my hundred pages of torn images and the ribbon of words together in one huge patched-together rectangle up on the wall of your classroom? Why did you say to the stunned girls sitting there, "Now this is a true artist's book"?

le raclement
des coquillage
au
fond

les
enfants

e faire bien comprendre
is son geste est muette;
se it affet est muette;
yeux fixés sur
rede . N e lui
exprime ses
ntiments pour elle .
lui explique la
sion que leur
amène .

Earlier, a man dropped by. His name is Janvier. He teaches auto mechanics to the grade elevens in the vocational program. Ulysses met him by chance in the cafeteria.

The god of engines has asphalt-colored skin and a broad, teasing smile. Ulysses' puzzle of engine parts struck him as so funny that he put his hands on his hips and threw back his head. His giant laugh bounced off the walls.

Ulysses waited, worried.

Janvier stopped laughing finally, shadow punched Ulysses in the ribs, and the two pals set to work.

I left the workshop with Tripod to run through the frozen vacant lot. Not only are Ulysses and I not talking, now he has a friend and tutor.

What if it works, the Great Plan and all that, what becomes of me? There's a bitterness in my mouth, like bile.

I grab Tripod by the scruff of the neck, kiss the top of his head, pat his undercoat, gather him into my arms. "We're good, just the two of us, right, puppy?"

Sitting on a cement post in the middle of the vacant lot, I write all this to you, Jeanne, in the notebook spattered with salty stains, my fingers numb with cold.

I use the dolly to move boxes into row five, the row for totally useless objects, figurines, trinkets and Christmas decorations. Made in China. Made in Taiwan. Made in India. Made in Turkey. Made in Indonesia.

I've heard that ten-year-old girls are sold into prostitution in Indonesia. Little boys too. In Latin America, rail-thin children roam big city dumps, collecting scraps of food. In Africa, boys become child soldiers. My mother tells me I watch too many sad news stories on TV, creating unnecessary anguish, and that I should focus on school, she wants me educated and making a good living when I grow up, but I know she sends a monthly check to an organization that builds schools in the poorest countries of the world. She never talks about it.

I can't help thinking about them, those exploited children of the world, as I line my shelves with shepherds and their sheep, cowboys waving their hats, plastic garlands of holly. I'm thinking of Christmas, which I hate, when my manager comes up behind me, orders me to follow her into the warehouse at the back of the store. Her tone gives off a bad vibe. Did I forget a box or something?

"Two employees saw you stealing merchandise," she begins.

Oh no! It was just a game. I clench my hands into fists, breathe deep, try to look tough. It doesn't work. I whimper like a small dog with its tail between its legs.

"I brought almost everything I borrowed back, except for a blue bowl and a figurine. I'll pay you. They're worth two dollars plus tax."

"You're fired. Consider yourself lucky I'm not calling the police."

This time, I raise my head. Through clenched teeth, I tell her, "You're paying me under the table. Less than minimum wage. You can't turn me in."

I rip off the white smock and throw it in her face. I spin on my heel, leave through the alley. Two dollars and thirty cents. I spit on the graffiti-covered brick wall. I won't say anything to my mom or anyone else as usual.

There you go, Jeanne. When you do stupid things, there's a price to pay. But I wonder why oil companies and the destroyers of boreal forests and the factories pouring poison into waterways and the people selling kids aren't punished. Tell me, Jeanne, do you know why?

Sunday afternoon. Ulysses isn't here. I'm sitting under the color table. He left me a note. "I have to go to my dad's for a birthday on Sunday. See you."

I scribble on the floor with a bit of chalk. I scribble and scribble, circles, squares, bubbles. Time stands still. He took Tripod with him. Bad idea. Tripod is as much mine as his. Suddenly, I feel an urge to bite. An urge to scream, demolish something. I jump up, cross the chalk boundary. Kick his caravan. I retrace my steps, run toward the color table. Ah-ha! I grab the pot of red, rip off the lid — just wait and see what your Caboose looks like when I'm through with it! I feel a cry of death and crime rising.

The double doors bang open. Tripod bounds toward me.

"I didn't stay long at the party. I missed the workshop," says Ulysses as he walks toward me.

He's brought two big pieces of chocolate cake in plastic wrap. He sits on the dividing line. So do I. I'm no longer the least bit angry. We look at each other, embarrassed.

"Are we making peace?" I ask.

"Ummm, yeah."

"Whose birthday was it?"

"Mine."

"Oh … Happy birthday. Did you get any presents?"

"Yup. Money."

He fights with the plastic wrap, manages to extricate both slightly squashed pieces. He hands me the bigger one.

"Damn blended family," he sighs. "I could have strangled a couple of them earlier."

"What are your parents like?"

"My mom's had a new boyfriend since last summer. He lives at her place. My dad just bought himself this year's car."

"Do you travel back and forth between their apartments every other week?"

"Yeah. Shared custody."

"Do you have brothers? Sisters?"

"Yup. You could say that. One half-brother. A quarter-sister."

"Which one did you want to strangle?"

Ulysses grimaces before answering. We're content, sitting facing each other holding our pieces of cake.

"My dad's living with his third girlfriend since the separation. They just had a baby. His girlfriend had another kid with some other guy before. Every second week, I live at my dad's with the girlfriend's daughter and the baby, who's my half-brother. My mom lives with an old friend of my dad's. He has a son. I can't stand him. The son. Huge arms, tiny brain. Today for my birthday, there was a big party with the whole blended family. Everyone thrown in one big basket. We're supposed to love each other. I just found out that for the last two weeks the huge-armed-tiny-brained son of my mom's boyfriend has been dating my dad's girlfriend's daughter. They were making out right there in the kitchen. Crazy, isn't it?"

"I don't have that problem. My mom and I never have anyone over."

"Lucky you! Every six months, my mom introduces me to the newest love of her life. 'Be nice to him, I love him!' My parents get bored fast. They change partners like they change cars. Or dishwashers, because the newest model doesn't make as much noise. They pay for ski lessons, English lessons, a new computer for me. But I feel so alone in their world …"

"My mom always has new boyfriends too. And I lost my job at Dollar Magic yesterday."

We keep on talking about our lives as we take tiny bites of our cake to make it last longer. Tripod licks our fingers. Ulysses wipes a chocolate smudge off my chin.

Tripod is the cutest dog ever. He walks lopsided and runs crooked, Ulysses and I play with him in the vacant lot every day, coming inside when it gets too cold. We talk and talk and for me, who's never really talked to anyone but you, Jeanne, and not for very long at that, it feels so strange. We're trying to see the world more clearly and ask all kinds of questions. Yesterday, it was "Why do humans keep making babies when everyone says the planet is going to die because of global warming and the way we're wasting water and destroying forests? And why are there so many lost children in orphanages, youth shelters, on the street?"

This morning, the conversation takes an abrupt turn.

"I saw you reading palms at Halloween."

He holds out his hand. I take it, kind of plump but big and strong, warm. I examine the network of lines and the image I see shakes me to the core. I can't look away. I fold his fingers into his palm and give him back his hand.

"So?" asks an impatient Ulysses, breathing hard.

"Nothing. I don't see anything. Maybe it only works on Halloween ..."

I lied. The image was clear, distinct. There was no doubting what I saw. In all her fragility, all tender, in surrender, my upside-down girl slept in the palm of Ulysses' hand.

The worst part, Jeanne, is I'll never let a man make love to me. Not even Samuel. Especially not Samuel.

That man in my room tried to get me to put his penis in my mouth, remember, Jeanne? The girl in layers will spend her whole life alone with her disgust and her fear.

Jeanne, I was heading to the library at four when he caught up to me, took hold of my arm. "Come grab a fruit juice or something at Café Lézard in the shopping district. I want to talk to you."

So I say nothing, follow him down the streets of the neighborhood, never taking my eyes off my black ankle boots.

We sit at the back, there's almost no one in the café. I order a mint herbal tea and Samuel orders a cappuccino. The waitress likes his looks — I can tell by the way she smiles when she comes back and sets his cup down in front of him.

Jeanne, it was awful, my heart wracked with pain.

Across from me, he stirs his cappuccino and sighs.

"Lots of people at school are saying you're in love with me. The idiots think it's a big joke."

"I know," I say, a huge lump in my throat. "It makes me sound crazy. Delphine spread the rumor that rag girl's in love with the best-looking guy in school. She thinks you belong to her, since she's the best-looking girl."

"Hmmm …"

"Are you into her?"

He stares at me for a second with charcoal eyes. "I'm not into Delphine. Or you. Or any girl."

A knife straight to the heart.

"I'm into guys. I never talk about it because if the Vandals found out, they'd beat me up in a washroom or outside school. You know what they're like."

I just about fall out of my chair. I'm going to shatter into a million pieces. Instead, I blush, I stutter, "Oh, sorry, I didn't know …"

Samuel just smiles. As if a weight has been lifted. I don't know where to go with this conversation, my tattered love story, so I stammer out the first thing that crosses my mind. "Is the tattoo on your neck to attract guys? Some kind of secret sign?"

He smiles again, nods. I have nothing else to say to him. We sit in silence.

I don't realize it right away, but I'm gradually starting to hate him. In his too-soft voice, he adds, "You're a special girl, the way you dress, the anger tinged with worry in your eyes, your shyness. Each in our own way, we're different from the others. School is hard for us."

I fume, "So what? If you're looking for friends, go talk to the lesbian girls!"

I grab my backpack and make an exit, boots stomping, hair bristling. I run past all the shops on the street.

Oh, Jeanne! I was such an idiot! The worst part is that deep down, I knew it. He never harbored secret thoughts for a girl.

My mom didn't go to work tonight — her voice was hoarse and scratchy. I like it better when she disappears into the night, I feel lighter, freer, I can run to the workshop and meet up with Ulysses where we can talk about us by the heater the way nomads used to by the fire a long time ago. I feel good in the workshop amid the chaos of ideas and secrets, but my mom has laryngitis and won't be going to work.

In pajamas, her hair up in a ponytail and a cup of hot lemon-and-honey water in her hand, she sits in the living room with Pandora's box on her lap.

It's her memory box. I never go looking for it on the top shelf in her closet, my mom is the only one who occasionally glances through what's inside. Every time, she says, "I'm organizing the pictures." I know her "organizing" has more to do with nostalgia.

I shut myself up in my closet-bedroom to ruminate, lying on my back, my hands crossed behind my neck. I almost never think of Samuel anymore. The fire in my belly died out almost as fast as it was lit. He was nothing more than a picture of an actor or a rock star. He wasn't real. I couldn't care less about Samuel. I'm sure Delphine doesn't know his secret. Time passes slowly, I miss Ulysses, my mom coughs in the living room. I don't like her Pandora's box because an entire year is missing, the year of her unfitness and the foster family.

Suddenly, she bursts into my room, trailing the smell of camphor.

I groan, "You have to knock first. Your tiger balm makes me sick." She's barefoot, her cheeks red with fever, and she looks like a little girl. I don't like that. Who needs a little girl for a mother? Normally, she's all made up when she goes out wearing stiletto heels and a miniskirt, her barmaid costume, but now, in her flannel pajamas, seriously.

She's holding a picture in her trembling hand and whispers in her rasping voice, "Look, sweetheart." Something she normally never does. We both tend to keep our distance.

I sigh as I take the picture. I don't know what I'm looking at, a blur of gray, black and white.

She sits on my bed, points to an indistinct shape through the fog. It looks, I don't know, like a big-headed fish or a tadpole or something. She adds, "That's you in my womb."

Me in her womb? I stare at the tiny fish. I spot a side fin that looks like a fist. I look up to meet her gaze. The tenderness in her eyes makes me want to hit her in the face.

"I was so happy to be pregnant with you. I couldn't wait to meet you, protect you and help you grow."

She leaves the ultrasound with me and shuts the door gently on her way out.

I spend several long minutes studying the secret picture my mom gave me, the little fish all curled in on itself, drifting in a water-filled pouch. It's hard to believe or even understand how that can be me since no memories remain of that floating time.

The five-centimeter-long fish will become a baby, then a little girl who'll be abandoned. Later, they'll come get her from the foster family, and the little girl will never again believe that her mother loves her.

Rage and pain bubble to the surface, I can no longer hold them in, I jump up, my door slams open against the wall, I run into the living room, park myself in front of my mother and her Pandora's box and yell with all my might, "You didn't keep your promise! You didn't protect me! You took drugs instead! You left me all alone! I thought you'd never come back!"

Jeanne, she doesn't even try to defend herself. She listens to me as I stand there trembling, screaming and sobbing while she sits on the living-room carpet.

When I stop, out of breath and words, she looks up and murmurs, "Forgive me, my little girl."

We don't budge for minutes that stretch into eons. We hold our breath. We don't know what's next. Will we rip each other apart with our fingernails? Will I spit in her face?

She opens her arms. "Come," she whispers.

I take a step, one single step. I trip. Mom catches me and gathers me onto her lap, I'm as big as she is, I overflow everywhere, my arms, my legs, I hang on to her neck.

We cry together, waves of salty tears that ebb and flow, ebb and flow, a giant tide of tears. "I missed you so much."

After many hugs, tender words and a pile of damp tissues, followed by more hugs, we calm down and realize we're starving. My mom picks up the phone, orders in a veggie pizza, and happiness hits us both.

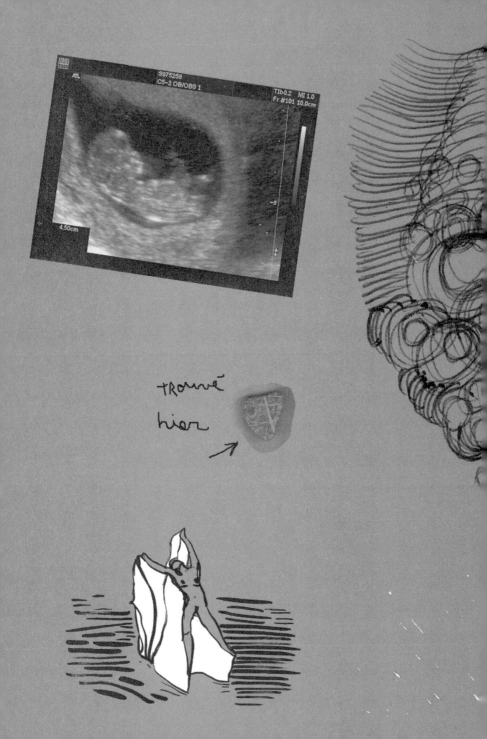

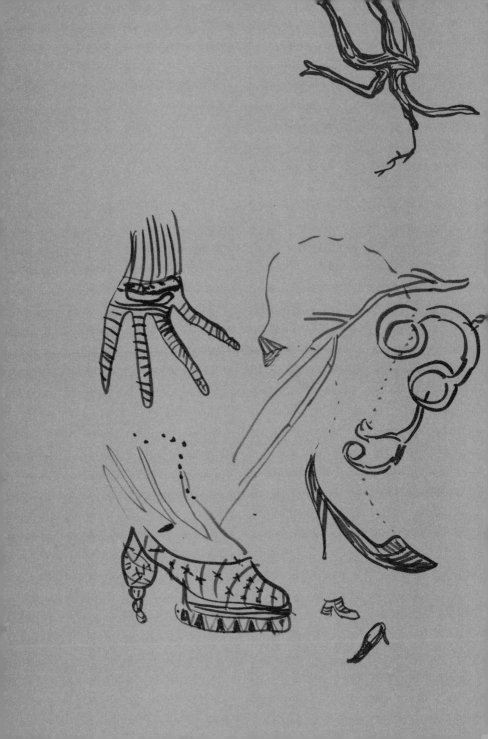

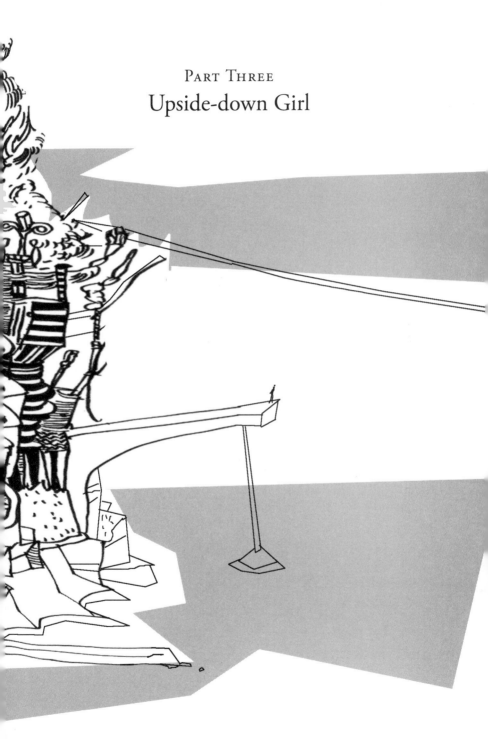

PART THREE

Upside-down Girl

When I look at the two of us, Ulysses and me, here in the workshop-refuge, I don't know what to think. We're so different from the others at school. We don't resemble anyone. We came up with our own first names. We live part-time in a secret squat where we've built a nest and drawn our guardians, where I sketch, where he rebuilds a motor with Janvier's advice. We feel so much less alone that sometimes we're almost happy, our souls soar and we dream — Ulysses of traveling, me of my upside-down girl. Our three-legged dog is ecstatic. The three of us cross the boundary so often that the chalk line fades more every day.

We would love to save other animals from dying. Did you know those beautiful burrowing owls that live in the Biodôme are an endangered species? That belugas are being poisoned to death in the river estuary? That the solitary wolverine may have already disappeared forever, its vast territory eaten up a little more each day by loggers? And what will happen to us humans? We don't know. We have no idea, Jeanne.

The outside world seems so inhospitable, and life at school has gone from bad to worse. For starters, a couple of Vandals have started pushing Ulysses around again. He shrinks away. He hugs the walls. I can't be in love with a guy who's scared of everything. But I can be his friend because he's like me. We are the race of the terrified. So sometimes in the workshop, I let him tell me how the Vandals circle him. He tells me that while it's going on, cold sweat trickles down his back, then his legs turn to jelly. He pictures them armed with machine guns.

When our angst ramps up, we look at our two unarmed warriors on the wall. Lately, they've been silent. Yesterday morning, we saw footprints in the fresh snow as we made our way across the vacant lot to the workshop-refuge.

I suggested Ulysses tell an adult at school about the Vandals elbowing him and calling him names, and he said, "Who could I talk to?" I did a quick mental scan and saw a parade of adults — the shrink who changes every month, the principal with barricaded lips, the old teachers on the verge of collapse, the teachers who pretend school is a great place where they have the privilege of transmitting knowledge — and I knew, deep down, that there was no one to share our fears with. I said, "You've got to arm yourself." I meant with courage, but Ulysses thought I meant with a gun. He said, "I don't want a gun." Then I had a brilliant idea, "Talk to Janvier."

That's where we stand, Jeanne. I'd so love to see you on TV again, it would do me good since where I'm concerned, even though girls don't resort to physical violence, their words hit hard. I haven't seen Samuel again. I don't think it was love I felt, just some kind of vertigo.

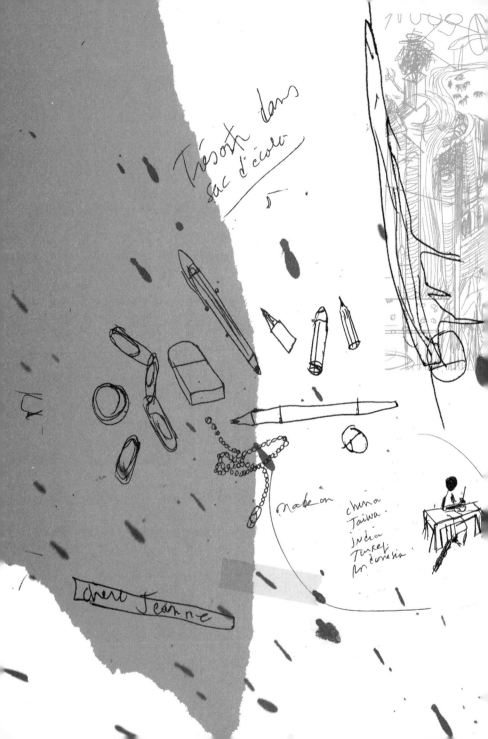

Our French teacher has assigned a three-hundred-word project. Help, Jeanne! I've already told you I'm hopeless at spelling and grammar. I'm also paralyzed by any blank page, I have terrible marks, and the margins of my written assignments are littered with comments in red: "You can do better. Use your imagination. Study the rules for past participles again."

It's only here in my ink-blue notebook that my chicken scrawl flows, as if in the notebook's secrecy, I've developed a mysterious power. Here, words come to me. They feel free and wild. They slide, jump, swim, tumble, cluster together, create astonishing sentences and speak of everything and nothing. I even write backwards. AILEHPO.

The project is to dig through our past in search of an old memory and bring that memory with all its details onto the page, then give it a title. I have no desire to delve into my past. But maybe I, who never writes or draws and barely speaks at school, can try it out here in the blue notebook?

I'm so little. It happens after a snowstorm, the street is white and clean. In my memory, I'm bundled up in my snowsuit, I can't move either my arms or my legs or even turn my head. A long wool scarf is wrapped around my forehead first, then over my mouth and nose, leaving only a slit for my wide-open eyes. My mom has settled me into the small wooden sled with the baby-blue fleece blanket to protect me even more from the cold.

We're off to the park, it may be early on a Sunday, since everything is still. At any rate, the snow removers, with their giant plows, their snow blowers, their trucks and sidewalk plows, haven't been to our street yet. I listen to the rasp of the sled's runners as they glide effortlessly and the rhythm of my mother's steps sinking into dry snow. Nestled in my shell, I watch her hips sway to the cadence of her walk and the sleeve of her coat, her leather mitt holding tight to the rope pulling me, her little girl, onward. The sled tips back as it passes over a mound of snow, and for a second, all I see is blinding sky.

It's all there. I just need to write a clean copy. My text isn't long enough, only 207 words. But happiness never lasts long, it's over in the blink of an eye, a warm smile. Only to turn into nostalgia for what has been and gone.

As for the title, I looked up a word in the dictionary to describe the feeling I had writing down my memory. I found this: dazzlement. Sounds nice, doesn't it, Jeanne?

Giotto blue
Nordic-lake blue
indigo blue
forget-me-not blue
salty-fog blue
Dutch-earthenware blue
winter-sky blue
fridge blue
blueberry blue
fall-mist blue, like your eyes, Jeanne
ocean blue, like Ulysses' eyes
melancholy blue
lavender blue
slate blue
frost blue
abyssal blue
starlight blue
bruise blue

The ocean's waves rock the upside-down girl. Maybe one day, given enough time and space and only the soft touch of fingertips on her skin, she'll make love. I want her back.

Ulysses and I talk more and more about whatever crosses our minds, words jostle, rush to be heard. This morning he told me about his deconstructed and reconstructed family, not unlike a house in ruins where certain spaces are livable, others not. I spoke some about mine, no half-sister or quarter-brother, no grandmother or uncles or cousins, just me and my mom, the night-shift worker desperately searching for a man to love.

"Do you ever see your dad?" he asked softly.

"No. I don't know who he is. I think even my mom might not know ..."

Ulysses brought his hand up toward my cheek. Pulled back. Intimidated by the almost-caress, I stammered, "Do you want a family when you're older?"

"I'd like someone to travel with."

"Why?"

"You see more and better when someone crisscrosses the world with you."

"I'm the opposite. Whenever someone gets too close, I can't see a thing. It sets off a racket, I can't hear myself think anymore, I don't like anyone getting too close. Touching me."

"Too bad …" said Ulysses.

Yes, too bad.

I just found out, Jeanne, the word spread at breakneck speed through the school. I hid out at the back of the library, alone, I need to write to you to calm down, to understand, it's just too awful. Last night, one of the lesbian girls swallowed all the pills from her parents' medicine cabinet. They pumped her stomach out in the hospital and she didn't die. Everyone's whispering in the halls, on their phones, by the lockers, at the back of classrooms that she couldn't take all the taunting and scornful looks anymore. They say she's only been with her girlfriend for a short while, before that she was into boys. People are saying all sorts of things, that she planned her suicide, wasn't strong enough to feel so different, that …

Oh, Jeanne, I feel like running to the hospital, finding her room, taking her hand in mine and whispering in her ear, "I'm here." I want to find Samuel, who I haven't seen since that day, and tell him, "It's okay if you're gay," and the girls wearing headscarves, "Modesty's okay even if I prefer my hair wild and free." Right here, right now, I want to reassure everyone whose lifeline is fragile, everyone who belongs to the race of the terrified.

I want to run to Ulysses, plant myself in front of him and stammer through my tears, "I'm sorry for all the mean things I said. Forgive me for 'You're fat, you've got a fat ass, fatso, I don't like obese guys, you disgust me.' Don't commit suicide, you hear me? Don't die. I need you, Ulysses, I need you so much, my friend. You're not fat, it's just baby blubber that hasn't melted away yet."

Ulysses! I've got to find him right away! Right away!

Scaredy-cat Ophelia didn't dare run to Ulysses or to any of the others living in fear. But every morning when I wake up, I think of them. They live inside me. Along with all the stray cats and dogs, all the children abandoned to foster families, orphanages, refugee camps.

Ulysses finally confessed his fears to Janvier, who told him, "The Vandals only respect brute strength, you need to build some muscle." So he meets Janvier in the school gym three times a week and lifts weights, runs and sweats like a race horse in training. In the workshop, he does push-ups and sit-ups. On my end, I brought in a CD player and play African music and dance while he exercises. It's fun.

Sometimes afterwards, we meet up in Caboose, Ulysses on the driver's side, me in the passenger seat and Tripod on my lap, and Ulysses dreams out loud about the future as he looks out the windshield. He told me about a sacred mountain in Tibet where people go once in their lives, and Mongolian deserts, and the traboules, secret passages in the city of Lyon, France. Ulysses believes the sound of certain words calls up images, like Savannah for instance, conjuring up for him white houses and the scent of magnolias. The warm beat of black music.

I don't know if I want to travel. Maybe I'd rather stay put under the writing-drawing table, reading stories. But I would like to see the icebergs once in my life. I confided as much to Ulysses, who then brought me a book full of nothing but pictures of icebergs. Some look like castles, others like huge tables. Using his maps, we found the route we'd take, it's quite far but not too far. In June, they pass close to the coasts like a mob, an army, on their way south, and farther along where the sun beats down, they vanish into the ocean.

Do you know the Hans Christian Andersen story about the little mermaid who lived in the ocean's depths and surfaced one day? She saved a young fisherman from a sinking ship, and propelling herself with her powerful fish tail, brought him back to shore. He looked so handsome lying unconscious in her arms, she fell in love, but mermaids are banned from approaching humans. With a heavy heart, she returned to her kingdom.

There in the depths, she cried for days on end and begged the spirit of the sea to change her tail to legs, till he finally agreed. She returned to dry land and walked to the young fisherman's village. Sadly, he was already in love with a beautiful young woman and didn't even recognize her.

She could no longer return to live among her people in the deep blue sea. So she swam out as far as she could and let herself sink. The little mermaid, who'd longed to be human for love's sake, drowned.

I am still and will always be afraid, Jeanne.

Without consulting each other beforehand, both Ulysses and I carried our trays over to the table where the lesbian girls sat in the cafeteria. The girl who tried to die had only been back at school for two days.

"Can we sit with you?"

They nodded and we didn't talk right away, just smiled. It was only later, once we'd finished eating, that one of the girls spoke to me.

"Every time I walk into art class, I look at your strange artist's book on the wall. It makes me think of all the people, animals and places there are everywhere on the planet. Your torn pictures make me shudder as if the world were in shreds …"

"I like the picture of the little girl with bricks on her head …" added the girl who didn't die.

I took the hand of this girl who had been saved from death. I hoped my hand would be as comforting as cats' fur.

"We're like the two of you. We feel different," said Ulysses.

We played mad dogs with Tripod this afternoon. We rolled on the ground and rubbed against each other, barking wildly. Then we drank the can of beer Ulysses had brought along. We split it fifty-fifty sitting under the color table draped in the blue sheet.

He told me he sometimes surfs the Internet to look at naked women. According to him, there are tons of close-ups of breasts and butts but very little expression on anyone's face. Sometimes little girls with flat chests and no pubic hair appear.

I shivered thinking of the man in my room, but Ulysses didn't notice and kept talking. He confessed he'd like to fall in love but doesn't know how. He has no idea how to approach a girl he likes.

I didn't tell him I'd like to fall in love for real too, but for that to happen, the boy would have to be tall, handsome and intrepid, plus he couldn't touch me because hands on my body hurt.

He said he'd like to fall in love with a girl whose breasts are the same size as the palms of his hands. Because cupping two breasts of just the right size is his dearest wish.

"I've never touched a girl down there," he murmured. "I've heard it's always moist and smells of vanilla between the labia. I don't know if that's true."

That night in bed, I used a finger to taste. It makes me think of cake.

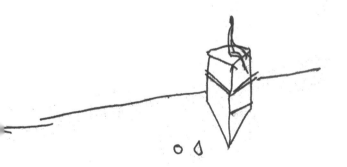

We speak hesitantly as if exploring words as shy and elusive as water running through our fingers. The blue cloth of my tent brushes against us. We stumble blindly toward things hidden and never spoken.

"Tell me again about the Internet women. The ones all the guys go to see, with plump butts and melon boobs."

"I don't like it. No one's in love on the Internet."

"I thought I liked a guy at school once. I was wrong. It was as crazy as falling in love with a movie star. Love was what I felt, but there was no one there."

We're silent for a moment. The ocean blue caresses our skin. I speak first.

"I don't want to be touched."

"So you've said …"

"I'm scared I won't like it but that I'll feel I have to."

"I'm scared of being turned down with insults. Like fatso, for instance."

"I don't think you're that big anymore," I say, blushing. "The better I get to know you, the skinnier you seem. I put you down because I was angry."

"Are you still angry?"

"No. Sad sometimes though. Before you came, I wanted to draw an upside-down girl on the wall."

"I know. I saw her outline. I brought you a gallon of primer, but you never redid your fresco."

"She's naked. I can't. I don't want her to be seen."

"Draw her. I won't look."

"Her thighs are open."

"I won't look."

"Her mouth is open."

"I won't look."

"Her breasts are pointed."

"I won't look."

"She's floating, she has no shell. If someone attacks her, she can't defend herself."

"I'll defend her."

"How would you do that?"

"Like the warrior on the wall."

"Oh …"

"Ophelia, one day will you take off your layers?"

"I don't know … No, never."

The others at school have noticed the way me and Ulysses are often together. We're not tongue kissing by the lockers or holding hands or anything, but they still laugh behind our backs. "Did you see the fat guy and the rag girl?" We don't give a damn because together we're stronger, and we exchange secret smiles with the two lesbian girls and a few others. A warm current of air passes between those of us with fragile lifelines, and without having to say a word, we know that if a Vandal, for instance, tries to mess with one of us, the others will come to the rescue.

I got the highest mark in art class and another really good one in French in spite of my spelling mistakes. The teacher wrote a note in the margin: "Your memory of the child nestled in a sled was very moving. Reading your text, I could see the winter light, I could smell the snow, I felt the burst of happiness."

Jeanne, I think you'd be proud of me. Who knows, maybe I won't flunk out this year.

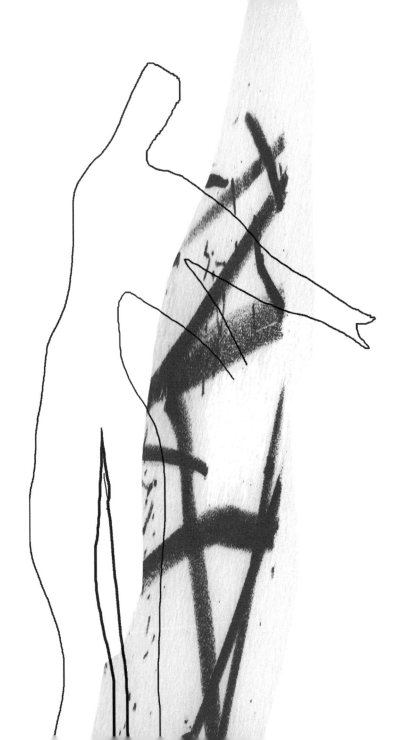

Earlier, out of the blue, just for fun, I peeled off a few layers, handed him a piece of chalk and said, "Would you trace the outline of my body? Like I did for you with the warrior?"

He hesitated for a second, and I was worried he thought I was too scrawny and ugly in my tight-fitting pants and figure-hugging tank top.

"Where? On the wall?"

"No. On the floor. Hold the chalk nice and straight."

"Where should I start?"

"Wherever you want."

Then I lie down on the cement floor and close my eyes. He doesn't start right away, later I hear him treading softly. I feel the chalk skim my left shoulder. He keeps tracing down my arm, my wrist, digs a path between my fingers.

"Hey! That tickles!"

"Should I stop?"

"No! Keep going."

I giggle and have an irresistible urge to wiggle around as he comes up under my armpit and a hair's breadth from my left breast on the way back down. He discovers the shape of my body as he continues down my leg and around my foot. Slowly, he heads toward my crotch. I don't move a muscle and keep my eyes closed.

"You okay, Ophelia?"

"Mmm …"

He's extremely careful, trying not to touch me, holding the chalk by the very end and barely grazing my clothes. He charts my other half, sketches the outline of my hair. He's hot. I feel all gooey. When he makes it back to my left shoulder, I stay perfectly still for a moment. I open my eyes. Sit up. Ulysses stands there in front of me, huge, chalk in hand.

Then he rushes back to his side of the erased border to assemble his engine parts. I get to my feet. The other Ophelia stays splayed on the floor, languid.

Jeanne, when he just about touched me with the chalk, I got shivers everywhere. Sometimes Ulysses can be handsome — when he takes off his glasses, his eyes are full of blue mist.

I'd like him to caress my breasts. I wouldn't let him kiss me. Or touch me any lower down. Just my breasts, as if your fingers were feathers, water, a warm breeze, a cat's whiskers. Don't pull my hair. Don't undo your fly. Don't rub against me like I was a doormat.

We circle around what we do and don't want.

Today in the silence of the workshop, today Ulysses won't drop in, he promised. He's leaving me alone with my desire to paint the upside-down girl.

I have all my tools at hand — the brushes, the colors, my various shades of blue in their glass jars. I start with the outline, it's easy enough, I know it off by heart. The graphite pencil glides across the white wall, my fingers tremble just a bit, yet I draw with confidence. First the face, calm, eyes closed, lips parted. Then her small pointed breasts, breasts like mine, her open thighs, her arms, her hands, supple and relaxed, her long fawn legs.

I stroke her with my big soft paintbrush. I move back and forth, covering both her and the wall with my array of blues, I caress her with blue, I wrap her in blue water so she won't fall. I'm happy to see her again finally, but a sadness wells up inside me because she's all alone in her aquarium, my upside-down girl, and I realize I want Ulysses to see her, to think she's beautiful and speak words full of desire to her. Not the words we hear at school, did you get a load of those big tits, that tight ass, that big tease, but words of endearment, my gorgeous fawn, my moonstone, my love.

Then I sit on the floor and look at her. Every once in a while I get up to add a bit of blue, a black line for her eyelid, red on her open lips, her nipples, her vulva. Fires that burn in the night.

My upside-down girl looks like a fish fetus in her water pouch, like Andersen's little mermaid, like Shakespeare's Ophelia.

I've got both good news and bad news. First off, Christmas is coming and the stores need extra staff, so I found a Saturday gig at the hardware store. I'm a sales-clerk-in-training in the paint department and am learning to mix colors for customers. It's fantastic! Did you know that to make four liters of luminous white, you have to add a half drop of orange and three drops of yellow? All the different nuances between white-blue, black-blue, mauvish-blue and turquoise-blue make my head spin!

Plus, I went looking with Ulysses for the broken hearts I'd left on random walls throughout the city. He took pictures of all the ones we found. "For your archives," he said, "because your hearts will disappear under other graffiti." He did the same for the two girls and the warrior back in the workshop.

So far, so good. I don't like the next bit as much.

"That way," he continued, "when we leave, you'll have a reminder of your frescoes."

"But … I don't want to go!"

"We'll have to one day. This doesn't belong to us. Someday, we don't know when, the owner's going to show up. He's going to want his place back. Hadn't you ever thought of that?"

"What about Caboose?"

"She's too old and broken to belong to anyone. Janvier helped me see there's no way I could get a license plate for her, even if she was mine. Caboose is an old clunker beyond repair. Her main purpose is to help me learn car mechanics and dream of trips with you."

"You knew about Caboose all this time and never said a word!?"

"Ophelia, what I'd really like is for you to come with me to see the icebergs one day."

This morning, I lead Ulysses into my underwater cave.

"Touch me, Ulysses. Touch my hand. Just my hand."

He murmurs how soft and supple my hand feels, each finger a marvel with its bones, twenty-seven bones per hand, the distal phalanx of my little finger so tiny and my hands so lovely and so's my hair ...

"Not my hair. Just my hands, Ulysses. Hold them."

I give him my hands. He kisses them. "Nails like pearly shells," he says. Then he says nothing more. Lets go of my hands.

"I'm too fat for you."

Jeanne, something terrible has happened. They came last night in our absence. They broke the lock. They ransacked the place. The color table was knocked over. Paint pots too, rivers of red running along the ground, curtains of blue, red and yellow on the walls. Caboose all dented, her windows smashed, the small plaster Buddha shattered. Graffiti slashing upside-down girl's body. Words of hate. They took a piss in all four corners.

Who are they? The Vandals? Others we don't know? They'll be back, and they'll beat Ulysses with their bare hands and stone fists, and maybe they'll kill him. They'll rape me. That's the way it always is whenever and wherever war breaks out. The men kill each other and the victors rape the women from the other camp.

Ulysses trembles in fear. Ulysses is incapable of protecting me.

I'm writing to you about our tragedy, sitting under the color table that we righted. Once again I draped it in the blue sheet and daylight filters through. I'm watching over Tripod. Ulysses is sitting alone behind the wheel of Caboose, and I know he's obsessing over his weakness. If a guy doesn't feel as valiant as a knight, he feels like a loser.

Here he comes. He steps out of Caboose, shoulders hunched.

"Where are you going?"

"To dig a hole in the frozen ground."

Jeanne, they killed the guard dog. They killed Tripod.

you licked my fingers, my face
on days full of sadness
on mornings of wild dancing

you laid your head in my lap
for hugs
whispered words

you ripped the night monsters to shreds
made their blood splatter
never backed down

my friend, my brother
your body rests in my arms
farewell, Tripod, farewell

We gathered our things together. We could no longer stay in the workshop. But where could we hide away to dream? Learn to touch without hurting each other? Explore our images of the world? Ruminate together? Hold each other close for warmth?

I cried as I folded up my underwater cave's blue sheet. Ulysses knelt on the floor, stony-faced, filling a garbage bag with his atlases, maps and travel guides.

They walked in through the double doors as if they owned the place. There were three of them, we recognized them, three Vandals from grade eleven.

I could think of nothing but rape. I felt like throwing up.

Ulysses slowly straightened up as they positioned themselves in front of him without saying a word.

A pale Ulysses took a step toward the one standing in the middle.

"You killed our dog."

"Your dog was a fucker. He bit me."

Ulysses grabbed his arm.

"No one kills animals. Not in my place. Get out of here."

The guy turned to look at his buddies. They were smiling, relaxed.

Ulysses loosened his hold on the guy's arm.

The Vandal in the middle punched him in the face. Blood spurted from Ulysses' mouth, his glasses flew off, but his body didn't budge.

"Get out."

"We want this place."

"You can't have it."

The Vandal on the left hit him. Ulysses didn't fall. He repeated, "No one kills animals in my place." The guy on the right stepped closer. Ulysses just took their blows, he didn't hit back. He stayed standing, legs like pillars and repeated, "Animals, no one kills animals."

The ugliest of the three turned toward me, a smirk on his lips. I screamed.

Ulysses pounced, his fist as hard as a hammer.

The Vandal lying on the ground, moaning.

Ulysses staring at his fist as though it didn't belong to him, saying, "Do you know the definition of vandal? Did you check in a dictionary?"

The other two looked at him, stunned.

"A brutal, ignorant destroyer," continued Ulysses as he helped the guy cupping his nose back to his feet.

Jeanne, they backed off.

They left.

On the back wall, the warriors shone in all their glory while Ulysses and I, still standing, trembled with fatigue and emotion. I padded toward him in my alley-cat way, handed him his glasses, which he stuffed into his pocket. I stood on tiptoe, he leaned over, and gingerly, I took his face in my hands. My lips brushed his, his lips pushed against mine. I half opened my mouth. A long kiss, neither of us moving.

This morning at school, everyone in the hall started whispering when Ulysses and I walked in holding hands. There was no ignoring Ulysses. He seemed taller. I'd say his true height.

We saw Janvier in the locker area. When he saw the pride in Ulysses' gaze, despite the two black eyes behind his glasses and his split and swollen lip, Janvier threw his head back and let loose his thunderous laugh. "Tell me," he said. But when Ulysses told him about Tripod's death, Janvier was no longer laughing.

"You have to tell the principal about the Vandals. Or the police."

"You know we're squatting there. I don't want the police showing up."

"They're dangerous. They killed your dog."

"They won't be back."

"They'll take it out on others."

"No, I don't want to."

End of story. We had our own idea. At noon on the dot, Ulysses met me in the cafeteria and together we went up to the student radio station. Samuel was there in charge of music, and when he saw Ulysses, he said, "You fought a Vandal, didn't you? You're pretty brave."

"No," answered Ulysses, "or not much anyway. Can I use the mic for a minute?"

Samuel agreed and stopped the music. Ulysses stood in front of the big window.

"Have you noticed the raccoon mask I'm wearing?" he asked, and his voice ricocheted off the cafeteria walls.

Down below, heads turned in his direction. A few students laughed.

"I learned something important yesterday … If people make fun of me for being too fat, too smart, too anything else, I don't have to believe them or hang my head. I don't have to let them intimidate, insult or threaten me. But that doesn't mean I have to be the first to strike or buy a weapon or gun people down. I just have to stay standing. That's what I learned yesterday. To stay standing."

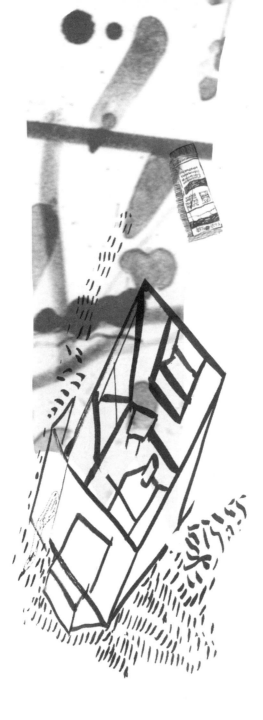

Dear Jeanne,

With everything that happened, me and Ulysses decided to come back to the workshop-refuge every day until Christmas vacation, in a week's time. I told him the letters locked in my blue notebook were written to you. He didn't seem surprised.

It's weird, but at school I no longer think our biology teacher, who asks himself and us so many questions, is all that bad. The lesbian girls gave me a hug after Ulysses' radio appearance. Before, I'd have thought they were getting too familiar the way boys do, but no, it's just a budding friendship. As for the Vandals I kept seeing everywhere, now I notice that there are actually very few of them. Ulysses says my perception has changed, and maybe he's right. I even found out that some of them have been arrested for selling drugs and carrying weapons. They won't be back at our school. Who turned them in? Janvier? The principal? I don't know.

On TV, I saw a doctor who cares for shattered families and judges no one, scientists concerned about our damaged planet, others who believe in acts of solidarity. But best of all was the woman who makes security blankets out of fleece, and drawstring bags with giraffe, teddy bear and sun motifs for abandoned kids moving from one foster home to another. I'm discovering the light that exists in certain people. I can count on them. Mostly, I can count on you, Jeanne, even if you don't know it, and Ulysses can count on Janvier, who's as dark as asphalt gleaming in the rain and full of joy.

I want to get even closer to Ulysses, who's so much braver than he thinks.

I lead Ulysses over to my blue underwater tent.

"Touch my breasts, please."

"Through all your layers?"

I take off my sweater big enough for two, my extra-large T-shirt. And finally, my tank top. My eyes are closed in anguish. He says, "Oh …" and reaches for me, I can tell because a wave of heat approaches, intensifies and I whisper, "Gently, please, gently, gently." He grazes one breast with his palm, just barely, then the other, then both and suddenly I go a little crazy, a lot crazy, my body arches, I want it all, I want it all right now, I want him to touch me everywhere but he doesn't and my stomach aches. "Again," I beg, panting like a puppy. "Touch me lower, my tummy and there, between my thighs. With your hands, there, there," and I'm transported to another world, like never before. "That's good, so good." My head drops back. "Hold me. Hold me. I'm falling," and his fingertips caress the moist and burning part of me. "Again!" then I lose all control, scream and scream, and he holds me. "Ulysses!"

His turn today.

We're naked in our cave, we've left our clothes outside. Sitting face to face, we look at each other for a long time without moving, I'm burning. He lies down on his back. I say, "Tell me what you want." He doesn't answer, so I start running my hand over his body, a millimeter above his skin. I name each part — shoulders, arms, hands, thighs, belly — but touch nothing and I see his penis harden.

"You won't move, Ulysses? I get to decide?"

"Yes."

"Close your eyes."

"They're already closed, Ophelia."

His penis is erect. His breathing is heavy. Gently, I run my fingers along its length. He groans. I stroke his chest. I brush my hands up his thighs. I press my lips where he feels the burning and he moans. "Ophelia," he murmurs, "Ophelia, again." I place my half-open lips against his and my fingers encircle and start to massage his penis gently, he moans with pleasure and his moaning swells, becomes an animal cry and I cry with him.

As of now, there are no more words.

We lie in our nomad's tent, my head on his shoulder, our arms and legs intertwined.

"Ulysses …"

"Hmmm …"

"That day in the library, when Jeanne came, you asked for her autograph …"

"Hmmm …"

"What did she write for you?"

"I know you're brave. I saw it when you dared to be vulnerable in front of the others."

Like an offering, I place a love note for Ulysses where the dividing line used to be.

under the girl's
layers,
a golden snake
dances
her joy in you

Sous les pelures de
la fille,
une couleuvre dorée
danse
sa joie de Toi

Our turn today.

Sitting cross-legged in the blue cave, we gaze on each other's body and face, our eyes caressing for the longest time. Ulysses asked about penetration, he'd like to today, and a wave of apprehension ebbs and flows because I know we might make a baby by accident. What if it hurts? I brought a condom.

He touches my cheeks, my eyelids, my lips, and the melting starts, a fire lights in my belly, I grab the condom and try to slide it on his penis. I laugh, embarrassed. Suddenly, I freeze. "It won't work."

"Let me do it today," he says, and I lie on my side. He caresses my small breasts, his body is hot, hot, his hands gentle, and the desire to burn with him returns. He guides my hand, I slide the condom on, he brings his sex close to mine, pushes lightly against my cleft. I lose it. "No! It'll hurt!" He pulls back, we both lie on our side, and I start to cry, my head buried in his shoulder, "I'm too scared Ulysses!" He mumbles, "It's because I'm fat."

We cry together. All desire is gone.

"Pass the ketchup?" asks my mom.

I do.

"Things not going well with your boyfriend?"

I jump up, my chair falls over, I run to my closet-bedroom, the door slams, tears flow.

She comes in without knocking.

"Go away! How did you know?"

"You've had a glow about you these past few days. And then … a pack of condoms disappeared from my dresser drawer."

I cry even harder. She sits at the foot of the bed, places a hand on my ankle.

"Is he kind?"

"Yes! He's kind, he's strong. It's just that …" and it all comes tumbling out, my confused fears, the man in my room, accident-babies, STDs, the workshop-refuge we have to abandon, love, risks, life!

"And you, Mom, always changing lovers."

She smiles, sadness in her eyes.

"You know what I'd like? Bring him home over the holidays. I'd like to meet the boy who makes my daughter glow."

Back in the blue cave, after caressing each other with our eyes and our hands and our mouths, everywhere that desire burns, everywhere that electric shocks intersect and crackle, we slip the condom on, and Ulysses says, "We don't have to," and I say, "I want to, I want this too," and he pushes gently, stops, "You guide it inside, I won't do anything," and I reach down, open up, he barely pushes and I open even more, the furnace kicks into high gear, he slides inside, deep inside, and I gently rock, him too, we moan, hold each other tight, move as one, suddenly faster, faster, and I cry out, him still inside me and me around him, and explode into fireworks.

Last day. The two of us face to face while our bodies burned, our eyes open all the while, until the very end, in the heart of the storm that shook us both. Giving myself over, lost, liquefied, disappearing into the ocean blue of Ulysses' eyes. At that moment I knew I'd been healed of all my fears.

Tu me léchais les doigts, le visage

les jours de peine

les matins de danse folle

Tu posais **TA** tête sur mes genoux

Pour les câlins

Les mots chuchotés

Tu as mordu à pleine gueule les
monstres de la nuit

Fait gicler leur sang

SANS RECULER JAMAIS   JAMAIS   JAMAIS

mon AMI, mon FRÈRE CHIEN
TON CORPS REPOSE DANS MES BRAS

ADIEU   TRIPODE   ADIEU

Dearest Jeanne,

Today we leave our workshop-refuge for good. We've repainted the walls white. Don't worry, I'm not sad. My girls live on inside me, they are my guides, they teach me that some times call for courage and strength, at others it's okay to give yourself over to the ocean's waves. We took one last imaginary trip in Caboose, all the way to the icebergs this time. They're gigantic, pure white with stripes of blue, and we'll go see them for real the summer I turn eighteen. We stood at Tripod's grave in the vacant lot, and he too lives on in me.

Over the last few days, I've talked to Ulysses about you and I decided to mail you both the ink-blue notebook full of words and sketches, and the poems and photos of broken hearts I slid inside. The bubble-wrap envelope has been bought. The stamps too. I chose snow-crystal stamps and stuck them along the edges of the envelope. Your address is printed in block letters with a permanent marker. I double-checked your postal code, there'll be no mistake. I'm using the front page to write you this note. The last note.

Jeanne, do what you want with our story, crazy and true, I'm giving it to you. Maybe it'll feel good to read an unfinished story where hope can be reconstructed still, because we have no idea what lies ahead.

Maybe you'll always want to keep this notebook on the bottom shelf of your bookcase, or maybe you'll want to copy my words onto your computer, who knows. You might correct my spelling or make a few changes so my words fit or sound better. Maybe you'll decide to let others read my story. I'd like that.

You were a candle in my dark night.

I send you warm hugs, as does Ulysses.

Ophelia

Charlotte Gingras started out as a young girl in love with all the stray dogs and cats she came across, then became a teen who dressed in black and devoured books. Later she became a teacher, then an artist. She now works full-time as a writer. Her novels *La liberté? Connais pas …* and *Un été de Jade* have both won the prestigious Governor General's Literary Award and have been translated into several languages. She lives in Montreal.

A well-known illustrator, graphic artist and engraver, **Daniel Sylvestre** has illustrated several picture books and novels, and he has been the artistic director for la courte échelle's poetry collection. His illustrations for *Rose: derrière le rideau de la folie* by Élise Turcotte won the Governor General's Literary Award, and his illustrations for *Ma vie de reptile* by Sylvie Massicotte were shortlisted for the same award. He lives in Montreal.

Christelle Morelli and **Susan Ouriou** are award-winning translators who were shortlisted for the Governor General's Literary Award for Translation as co-translators. Susan's translation of *Pieces of Me* by Charlotte Gingras won the Governor General's Literary Award. They both live in Calgary.